Murder, of course, is the great equalizer. And if the heavy hands of the cops had done nothing else, they had taught me one thing——that the responsibility of finding the killer was ultimately mine. The murder of a woman was now my affair. Somehow I was going to have to find a way to sink my respectable hands deep into the slime of sudden and violent death . . .

JOHN D. MacDONALD

YOU LIVE ONCE

A Fawcett Gold Medal Book
Fawcett Publications, Inc., Greenwich, Conn.

I have never awakened easily. I have always had a sneaking envy for those people who seem to be able to bound out of bed, functioning perfectly. I have to use two alarm clocks on work mornings.

The prolonged hammering at my door finally awakened me. I groped blindly for my bathrobe, and shouldered into it as I walked heavily, still drugged with sleep, from the bedroom of my apartment out through the living room to the front door.

I knew that it was a Sunday morning in May, and knew that I had a truly sickening headache, far out of proportion to the drinking I had done on Saturday night—two cocktails before dinner and two widely spaced highballs afterward. I wondered if I had been poisoned by something I had eaten. The headache seemed focused over my right ear in a tender area as big as an apple. My hangover headaches are aches that go straight through. And why the sore spot?

I opened my front door and squinted at the two men standing on the shallow front stoop in the bright morning sunshine. One was in uniform and one was not. Their prowl car stood where I usually park my car. I remembered where my car was.

"You Clinton Sewell?" the man in the grey suit asked. I said I was and they walked in.

"Were you out with Mary Olan last night?"

I sat down and looked up at them. I was afraid I knew what this was all about. "An accident? Is she hurt?"

Grey suit was spokesman. "What makes you ask that?"

"I swear she seemed all right to me. The night air straightened her out. She said she could drive and I believed her."

"You had a date with her last night."

"That's right. She played golf with some woman yesterday afternoon at the Locust Ridge Club. It was arranged that I'd meet her later, along with the Raymonds, and we'd have dinner there. There was a dance last night. I drove out about six, and the Raymonds arrived a little later. Mary had brought a change of clothing with her, and she was waiting in the cocktail lounge."

"When did you leave?"

"About two this morning. That was about . . . nine hours ago according to my watch."

"But you didn't take her home?" The uniformed man strolled over and looked in my bedroom, then the bathroom, and came back.

"No. She had her own car. She got a little high. Too high to drive safely. That made it complicated. I had my car there. It's still there, in fact. After an argument she agreed to let me drive her home. I was going to take a cab from her house, either back here or back to my car, whichever I felt like. I hadn't decided. We had the top down on her car. I got her almost home and she said she felt fine. She seemed to be okay. So I turned around and drove back here and got out and she went on home. Did something happen on the way home?"

"She never got home, Mr. Sewell. Her aunt got Mr. Stine, the Commissioner of Public Safety, out of bed this morning. That gave it a priority. I guess you know what the Olans and the Pryors mean in this town. Did Miss Olan say anything about going any place else?"

"No. She was pretty tired. She'd played twenty-seven holes of golf. We planned to go up to Smith Lake this afternoon and do some water skiing."

"Why did she drive you here, instead of back to your car?"

"She started to, but then we decided that she'd drive me on up to Smith Lake in her car today, picking me up here. Then when we got back to town late today, she would leave me off at the club."

They had both relaxed a bit. The one in uniform said, "It'll turn out she went to see somebody and stayed with them."

Grey suit shrugged. "Could be. Thanks, Mr. Sewell. Sorry we woke you up."

I stood in the doorway and watched them get in the prowl car, swing around and drive out. It was a beautiful day—bright, clear and warm. This would be my second summer in Warren, my second summer in the Midwest. I wondered what had happened to Mary. I wasn't particularly worried; she was unpredictable. I decided I would go up to the lake anyway, on the off chance that she'd show up. Some of her friends would be up there.

I was close to the phone when it rang.

"Clint?" It was the cautious voice of Dodd Raymond, my new boss.

"Good morning to you, Dodd. Do you feel as bad as I do? You had the lobster too, didn't you? Got a headache like mine?"

"Clint, have they asked you about Mary?" I could tell from the tone of his voice that he was speaking so that his wife, Nancy, couldn't overhear the call. I ached to call him a fool.

"The police were here. She didn't get home last night. She dropped me off here."

"I thought you were going to drive her home?"

"We had the top down. She felt better after a while."

"They phoned me. Her aunt told them she heard her say she planned to see us at the club. I told them she had a date with you."

"In a manner of speaking."

"Knock it off! I told them where you live."

"Thanks. So why didn't you phone me and tell me they were coming?"

"Clint, that damn phone rang twenty-three times before I hung up."

"Well, they don't know anything so far. She'll turn up. I'm going on up to the lake anyway. Will you?"

"I don't know yet. See you Monday if we don't."

He hung up. I went and opened the can of cold tomato juice, poured a high glass and laced it with Tabasco. I leaned against the sink and let it go down slowly. The headache throbbed over my right ear.

I thought about Mary and about my damn fool boss, Dodd Raymond. My dating Mary Olan was supposed to be misdirection, the way a magician operates. I wouldn't have stood still for any such fool arrangement had it not been for Dodd's wife, Nancy. And I had earnestly tried to follow Nancy's unspoken plea. Even last night when I had parked Mary's car in the dark driveway beside my apartment, turned out the lights and made an expansive pass. Mary had permitted herself to be kissed. But her heart wasn't in it. She was a highly exciting, and excitable, woman but I was just a good friend. She told me so. Emboldened by her intake of liquor, not my own, I had suggested that she leave Dodd alone. She hadn't gotten angry; she had just laughed. I had made another half-hearted try, but it had been ruined by some damn fool who had used my driveway to turn around in, lighting us up like a stage.

That had spoiled the mood. We'd planned the trip to the lake and I had explained to her my unique habits of sleep. After she'd promised not to use cold water if I wasn't up, I went and unlocked my front door and took the key out to her. The spare key was in the drawer of my desk. I made a mental note to take it with me to the lake.

I remembered that after I had gone to bed, in the few minutes before sleep fell on me like a woolly bear, I had gotten erotically fanciful about Mary Olan's coming in to wake me the next day. There wasn't a chance in the world that she would let me float up out of sleep and pull her down into my warm bed, but there was no law against dreaming.

In some ways I couldn't blame Dodd Raymond. Mary Olan is smallish but sturdy. I think I could span her waist with my hands. She is brown and rounded and firm. She has black, black hair and about all she does with it is keep it out of her eyes. She has a thin face, a wide mouth, black caterpillar eyebrows, a go-to-hell expression, limitless energy and several million bucks tied up in various trust funds. She has an air of importance. Waiters and doormen snap, pop and crackle when she lifts one finger, or one millimeter of eyebrow. In a faded bathing suit in the middle of Jones Beach she would still be unmistakably Somebody. She has an electric something that could disorganize the equipment in a research lab. Even the halfhearted kisses she had allowed me would each have melted an acre of perma-frost above Nome.

I had learned during the short time I had been dating her that her private life had been sufficiently lurid so that without the large bucks she could have been termed a bum. The trust funds relabeled it "eccentric" and "lively." There had been one marriage, an annulment, other escapades and scandals. Such knowledge did nothing for my self-esteem. Inability to make any kind of time with a virginal lassie is no stamp of failure, but the brushoff from a lively one causes what might be termed an agonizing reappraisal. She had begun to make me feel as virile and fascinating as a teaberry leaf. I kept telling myself it was singlemindedness that blocked my path. She had Dodd on her mind.

Perhaps today, I thought, she will arrive at that moment of awareness. And then Nancy Raymond will be happy again. Dodd will suffer and get over it. Mary will melt, and Sewell will munch clover.

I smacked my Tabasco lips, shed robe and pajamas, and headed for the shower. After five minutes of water—

warm, then cold, my head felt better, and I tested the resonance of the shower stall with a high-volume rendering of "April Showers." I scraped brown stubble from my face, brushed the brown brush cut, showed myself my teeth in the mirror and padded out for a judicious selection of sport shirt. The yellow one, I decided. And the new grey wool and Dacron slacks, and take along the white hopsacking jacket should we decide to eat out at one of those places at the lake.

I went to the closet to get dressed. It's a nice, roomy closet. There was sun in the room and light spilled into the closet when I opened the door. As I took out the grey slacks, I looked down and saw one brown female foot in a high-heeled gunmetal pump. I looked at it with the greatest blankness in my mind that I have ever experienced. My overcoat and topcoat were in the way. I slid them along the closet bar and looked down at the hideous, bloated, empurpled, barely recognizable face of Mary Olan. Her thickened tongue protruded from her lips.

The world stopped. I could hear traffic going by the house, hear a bird song in the elms. I could not look away from her face. It had the ugly, chilling, frightening fascination of an open wound.

There is no stillness like that special stillness of the dead. I shut the closet door slowly and carefully. The latch clicked. I sat on the bed. Though the room was warm, I was shivering. I went over to the bureau and took a cigarette from the opened pack. I wanted some way of finding out that it wasn't true. Yet I knew it was no trick of light, no aberration that went with the fading headache.

I sat numbed by the enormity of this thing. Staring at the closed closet door, I could see the horror beyond it. She could not be dead and she could not be in my closet—but she was there. I stubbed out the cigarette and opened the closet door again. I forced myself to kneel and touch her ankle. Her flesh was cold—a special kind of coldness. And within the closet, mingled with the musky scent of the perfume she used, there was the dank, cloyed odor of the dead.

After a time, I pushed more of my clothing out of the way and turned on the closet light. And I saw what was around her neck.

Back in the fall when I had purchased some shirts, an energetic salesman had sold me a red fabric belt with an arrangement of brass rings rather than a buckle. It wasn't the sort of thing I usually buy. I believe I have worn it twice. The last I had seen of it, it was hanging from a belt and tie rack on the inside of my closet door.

Now it was around Mary Olan's neck, the brass of the rings biting into the tender flesh at the side of her throat, the flesh above the belt darkened and grotesquely swollen. The long red end of the belt hung down across her shoulder and between her breasts. She still wore last night's dress, a sleeveless, strapless affair with a gunmetal top and full white skirt. She sat back in the corner of the closet, propped up, her head canted to the right. One leg was out straight—it was that foot I had first seen. Her other leg was sharply bent. Her white skirt had slid up her thighs exposing the white sheen of diaphanous panties contrasting with the dark tan of her legs. Her right hand was on the floor, palm upward, fingers curled. Her left hand was in her lap, hidden by the folds of the skirt.

I found after a time that I could look at her more calmly. The closet light glinted on one gold hoop earring. Careful examination told me nothing more than that she was dead, and had died by violence. These lips, hideous now, had been warm when I had kissed them. These arms had been around me. These brown legs had walked ahead of me, the white skirt swinging, and she had looked back over her shoulder, with a quick wry glint of smile. She had looked good last night, and she had known it.

I closed the closet door for the second time. The presence of the body was like an oppressive weight. I knew only that I wanted it out of there, wanted to take it out of my apartment and put it in some other place. I could not think clearly while she was there.

I thought of phoning the police and tried to imagine myself carrying off that particular conversation. "Two men were here asking about Miss Olan. I just found her in my closet, dead, strangled with my belt." I'd seen a lot of her lately and I'd been with her last night. I had been drinking, but I wouldn't be able to prove how little. The two officers could testify that I had been in bed, and was so hard to awaken that I could have been sleeping off a blind drunk. The door had been locked.

The alternative was just not plausible. I had gone to bed and gone to sleep. Somebody had brought her in. She had been alive when brought in, so she must have been strangled here. And I had slept through all of it.

Yet somebody had done just that. Somebody who had hated her, and me. Somebody who would like to have me as dead as Mary Olan. It was not good to think about that kind of hate.

I dressed slowly and made a pot of coffee. I drank the coffee too hot, scalding my mouth. The cup rattled on the saucer when I set it down. I could feel time passing while I struggled with my decision. I reached for the phone several times, but never quite got to the point of making the call. I did not dare face the police with the feeble, implausible truth. When I checked my watch I found to my surprise that an hour had passed since I had found the body. I believe it was that hour which weighed the scales. I told myself it was too late to phone the police now. I knew I had to get the body out of there.

Once I was able to face that as a specific problem, my mind began to work better. I mechanically made my bed and cleaned up the few dishes I had used, while I perfected a plan that should work properly. While I was making my bed, I found one thing that puzzled me. There was fine granular dirt on the pillow and top sheet. I wondered about it for some time, but I could think of nothing that could cause it. I brushed it off. There wasn't much of it.

When there was nothing else I could do, I decided that I might as well get my car. I certainly couldn't take the body anywhere on my back. If I was going to move it, I had to have a car. I phoned a cab and it arrived in ten minutes. I got the extra key from the table drawer, and went out, testing the lock on the door after it shut behind me.

The driver took me to the club, mentioning several times what a fine day it really was. My black Merc sat dozing in the sun. I drove it back to the apartment, my heart bumping. I expected sirens and a ring of prowl cars around the place. It was unchanged. Bees clambered over dandelions and it was shady under the elms of the side yard.

Back in the apartment I looked out the window at my car. Object: to get body from closet into trunk compartment of car. There was no guarantee that Mrs. Speers, my busybody landlady, wouldn't be watching from one of her many windows. The body must not only appear to be something else, I should be able to prove it was something else if questioned later. The body would have to be wrapped in something disposable. I had heard of the police using a vacuum cleaner on cars and then doing spectroanalysis of face powder and such like. And making identification from a single human hair.

I knew what I could use to wrap her up. In the back end of the car there was an old tarpaulin, a greasy mess. I had laid it under the wheels during the winter to get out of heavy snow. On the coldest nights I had kept it over the hood of the ungaraged Merc, a hundred-watt bulb on an extension cord burning inside the hood. I went out through my kitchen and looked at the collection of debris in the attached shed. Warren has garbage collection, but they do not take cans and bottles. You save those until you have enough to warrant a trip to the dump. I had a reasonable collection.

My plan was set and it seemed practical. I went out and backed the car up close to my front door. I opened the rear compartment and took the tarp into the house. I loaded a small cardboard carton with cans and bottles and took it out and put it in the rear compartment, well over to one side. Mrs. Speers appeared with her usual magic, materializing sixty feet away, strolling toward me, smiling, a big unbending woman in a black and white Sunday print, wearing one white canvas work glove and carrying a pair of small red garden shears.

"Going to the dump, Mr. Sewell?"

"I guess it's about time. Thought I'd drop some stuff off."

"Oh dear, do you think you could take mine too this time? Joseph forgot it when he did the yard work Thursday."

"Gee, I'd be glad to, but I've got a lot of my own. Tell you what, after work Monday I'll run it over for you."

"I don't want to put you out."

"That's okay. I'd do it today, but I'm going right on up to the lake."

"Joseph is getting so absent-minded."

She wanted desperately to have a nice little chat. It was too bad that she hadn't rented her apartment to someone she could have talked to. The woman was obviously bored and lonely. Her life had been busy with husband and kids. Now the kids were grown and had moved away, and the husband was dead.

"Monday for sure, Mrs. Speers," I said.

"You're so kind." She smiled and sidled off to snip something. I went in and shut the door. I spread the tarp on the floor in front of the closet and opened the door. I felt squeamish; I didn't want to touch her again. I went in and fumbled with the belt. I had to stop and then try again. It came loose and I slipped it off over her head and unloosened it the rest of the way. I found two hairs clinging to the fabric, two of her black hairs.

I brushed them off onto the tarp, rolled the belt up and put it in my top bureau drawer.

The next was the worst. She was sickeningly heavy. I got her by wrist and ankle. I tried to hold her out away from me, but she swung against my shins. Her free arm and leg dragged and her head thudded against the door frame. I put her in the middle of the tarp. She sprawled on her side, hair across her darkened face. I was breathing hard. I got my flashlight and carefully inspected the inside of the closet. I couldn't see anything, but the walls were smooth enough to take prints. I took a towel from the laundry bag and wiped the inside of the closet. It was good that I did because the damp towel picked up three more long black hairs that I had missed. I wiped it again and found nothing.

I picked up the four corners of the tarp, and joined them. She curled into a ball in the middle. Taking a good grip on the four corners, I picked her up off the floor with my right hand. She must have weighed somewhere around one twenty. I moved over to where I could inspect the sight in the full-view mirror. The tarp fit her body snugly and it was unmistakably a woman in a tarp. Nothing else. If I'd gone out with that, Mrs. Speers' eyes would have bulged like a Thanksgiving dinner.

I set her down and thought some more. Then I went through into the shed and came back with a paper bag of cans and bottles. I held the four corners up again and wedged the cans and bottles down between her body and the tarp so as to destroy the distinctive rounded outlines. I missed on the first try. The next time, after I had gotten some down around her hips, she no longer looked like a woman in a tarp. She looked like a tarp stuffed with angular junk.

After counting to ten I hoisted her off the floor again and walked through the living room and out the front door. Mrs. Speers was alarmingly close, snipping at a rose bush. I wanted the tarp to look as light as possible. I used every ounce of strength to handle it negligently, swinging it into the back end of the car, lowering it without too much of a thump. As I swung it I heard the old rotten fabric rip. I saw Mary's tan elbow sticking through the rip. I banged the lid down and did not dare look at Mrs. Speers.

"My, you *do* have a load," she said.

"Quite a load this time. I let it accumulate too long."

"Why, I thought you went last week!"

"I didn't take it all that time."

"This is certainly a lovely day to be going up to the lake. Do you go to Smith Lake?"

"Yes m'am."

"Mr. Speers and I used to go up there years ago. He adored bass fishing. He was never very lucky, but he loved to fish."

"I guess it used to be a good bass lake. There's talk of restocking it."

"It's nice that you have friends up at Smith Lake, Mr. Sewell, with summer coming on and all. It makes a nice change. Who are you going to see up there? Any of the old families?"

"Mary Olan invited me up."

"You don't say! Their place is one of the oldest places on the lake. It certainly is the biggest, at least it was the last time I was up there. You know, Mr. Speers and I used to know Rolph and Nadine Olan quite well. I mean we weren't *close* friends. When Mary was quite little my youngest girl used to play with her. Their tragedy was a terrible shock to this city, Mr. Sewell, they were so prominent."

"I haven't heard much about that. Mary doesn't mention it, of course."

"She wouldn't, poor child. I can remember it like it was yesterday, the expression on Mr. Speers' face when he read it in the morning paper. Nadine always seemed like such a quiet woman. Almost shy. Sensitive, too. And Rolph was so clever at business. They say she never has responded to a single treatment and she'll have to stay in that place the rest of her natural days. I suppose it's a blessing though that she isn't well enough to realize she killed her husband. Afterwards we heard that he had been . . . seeing someone else." Mrs. Speers blushed delicately. "I suppose that's what drove Nadine out of her mind. She was Pryor, you know. Willy Pryor was her brother. He went for a time with my youngest sister before he married that Myrna Hubbard. I understand Mary Olan lives with them."

"That's right."

"It's a wonder that Mary, poor child, survived the shock, finding her father's body like that. Well, if you're expected up there at the lake, you mustn't let an old woman hold you up with all her chatter and reminiscences. Give my best regards to Mary."

"I'll do that."

"I understand . . . I know this is none of my business . . . that Mary travels with a rather fast set. They say there's a lot of drinking."

"Quite a bit, I guess."

"Well, I suppose you have to forgive her. With that background and all. You really can't blame her if she's a little wild. Now you run along and enjoy yourself, Mr. Sewell."

I waved to her as I drove away and headed out toward the city dump. I drove as though the car rolled over eggs. A few minutes ago it had been a body, something I had to get rid of. Mrs. Speers' conversation had turned it back into Mary Olan, the girl I had kissed last night. My hands were wet on the steering wheel.

I had to go to the dump. If there was any question, I'd be checked on that. The Warren dump is east of the city. It is a very orderly dump with bulldozer-dug trenches. There was a pickup truck unloading, and a station wagon with a father and two yellow-headed sons further down the line. I parked way beyond both of them and backed up to the trench. Nobody could see into the back end of the car, and nobody was likely to

park right beside me. People seem to like privacy for
disposing of trash. I opened the trunk and took out the
cardboard box and heaved it into the trench. Then I
opened the tarp and took out the cans and bottles, trying not to touch her and trying not to look directly at
her. The sun caught the two big diamonds in her wrist
watch. I thought I could smell the odor of death about
her. I wrapped her up hastily, shut the lid, got back in
the car and drove away. As I came toward the station
wagon it was pulling out. I saw my chance to be remembered. There was plenty of room to swing around him.
Instead I leaned on the horn, a long heavy blast. The
man and his two sons turned and stared at me with indignation and disgust. I gave them another blast, glaring
at them, and they drove away.

Back on the highway, I turned toward town. I had to
go down into town to catch the highway that leads north
into the hills of the lake country. There seemed to be an
exceptional number of police around for an early Sunday
afternoon. I drove over the bridge in heavy traffic
headed north. A mile and a half north of the river I
passed the Warren Tube and Cylinder Division of Consolidated Pneumatic Products, Incorporated—my employ-
er. The place is six years old, cubical, landscaped and
sleekly efficient. I rode by my place of employment
with her body in the trunk compartment.

I have never driven so carefully. It was like the extra
care you seem to use when you cross a street while
carrying a batch of expensive phonograph records. I had
visions of what could happen if somebody smacked into
me just hard enough to spring the trunk open. The more
care I used, the more narrow squeaks I had. The road
was crowded with damn fools, all of them in a hurry.

Once in the hills, I was in an area where many small
roads branched off to small lakes. I took one of the less
traveled ones. It was black narrow asphalt, lumpy and
extensively patched. It climbed over steep crests and fell
into crooked valleys. I had met no car as yet and I

looked frantically for a turnoff. I braked hard when I saw an old lumber road, a faint trace leading off to the left. Leaves and branches scraped the sides of the Merc as I turned into it. I drove about three hundred feet. I was well out of sight of the road.

I got out and listened to the silence. A bird sang and a fly circled my head with a self-important buzzing. I decided I had best not think about flies at all. I heard a car motor. It took a long time to come close, but after it went by the sound faded quickly. I saw no glimpse of it between the spring leaves. I could hear water running somewhere nearby. The woods had a spring smell of dampness.

I knew I had to get it over with. I opened the trunk, pulled the tarp up around her and lifted her out. I dragged the tarp over to the edge of a small drop, let go of two corners, holding the other two, and rolled her out. She tumbled down over the edge, rolled over three times and came to rest with her back to me, supported by a small pine tree. A frozen juice can I had missed rolled out with her and went on down the slope. I went down and got it. There could be a fingerprint on it. I tossed it into the back of the car. Then I went and looked over the edge again. I could see no clear footprint. That made me think of tire prints; I remembered reading that they could identify tire prints. I looked and found two places where they were clear. I could avoid those places on the way out. I got a stick and gouged the prints out.

Next I folded the tarp as small as I could get it. I walked deeper into the woods and found the rotten stub of a birch tree with a big hole in the side of it, about seven feet off the ground. I stuffed the tarp down in there and it didn't show at all. I went back and looked at her again. She looked awfully small, like a child dressed up in woman's clothing.

The pine shadows were heavy, and her white skirt had an almost luminous look. Twigs and bits of leaf clung to her skirt where she had rolled over and over until the tree caught her across the middle. She was draped across the tree, white skirt pulled tight across dead hips.

I stood and looked down at her, wanting to leave, but immobilized, caught up in recent memory. It had been an evening when, as usual, we had been out with Dodd and Nancy. Dodd had been surly and Mary Olan had been overly gay, as though taunting the three of us. After Dodd and Nancy went home, Mary had wanted to go on. We hit a lot of little highway places. As she became drunk, she grew more affectionate. It was clear that she was annoyed at Dodd. I felt that I might become an instrument of her revenge, and I was willing.

We stopped at a grubby, forlorn little motel forty miles from town, and the fat clerk, with insinuating sneer, asked for ten dollars. Once we were in the shabby room, she lay across the bed face down and cried for a long time. She wouldn't tell me why she was crying. When I asked her if she wanted to leave, she didn't answer. When I tried to kiss her, she pushed me away. I sat and smoked and waited her out.

She dried her eyes, cheered up, kissed me lightly and went into the bathroom. I heard the shower running for a long time, and then I heard the sound of a fall. I went in and found her on the floor, half in and half out of the shower. She had hit her head. I carried her, utterly limp, back to the bed.

Her body was brown, smooth, flawless. Her pulse felt strong and slow. I brought towels and dried her. The mark on her forehead was minor, and I wondered if she was faking. I took her in my arms, but she was completely without response. I suspected her of faking, and was tempted to call her bluff by possessing her. Absolute helplessness brings out an atavistic streak in anyone. Yet there was the chance that she had actually passed out, or that this was some sort of hysterical seizure.

And, delectable as was her body, helpless as she was,

I could not be that cold-blooded about it. I found her crumpled clothing in the bathroom and hung it up. After I had covered her, I got into the other bed.

Dawn was grey when she shook me awake. She was dressed, impatient to leave, and in a mood of controlled fury. She did not speak on the way back. The sun was coming out as I left her near the Pryor driveway. She walked toward the house without speaking, without looking back. The next time I saw her she acted as though it had never happened. I never got that close to her again.

Now, standing there in the wood's gloom, looking down the slope at her slack body, I thought of that other time. It was a chill body now, not steamy warm from the shower. I saw the shape of her hips, the roundness of her arms, the smooth tan of her shoulders. Never again, for anyone, would there be the avid response, the controlled silken surgings of that body, the wide mouth warm. It was death and it was waste. I thought of myself and of the incalculable date of my own death. I shivered and turned away from her and drove away. I was troubled and frightened. And sad.

chapter 2

Back on the main highway at fifty miles an hour, each second took me almost seventy-five feet further away from the body of Mary Olan. I told myself I felt fine. I told myself I'd functioned superbly. I told myself I was a hell of a fellow indeed. Actually, I felt shamed and rotten and sick inside.

I stopped at a roadside place where the siding was made of neat perfect artificial logs. I went in and sat at the counter, looked at the spotted menu and smelled the short order grease. My stomach closed into a knot. I ordered hot black coffee.

I kept seeing her. Last night she had walked in front of me, her compact, muscular little rump jaunty under the hang and swing of the white skirt, black hair bounding against the nape of her neck. Now there was a pine tree across her middle, and the first person to walk in there would see the white skirt and the brown legs on the slope of the hill—something used up and thrown away.

Her death had not been dignified, stowed in my closet, but I felt that I had added a further indignity. I had in some macabre way allied myself with her murderer. Between the two of us we had despoiled Mary Olan.

The conversation with the police—the phone call I could have made—no longer sounded so idiotic. Certainly they would have given me a rough time, but it wouldn't have lasted long. Where was my motive? They had their lab methods, their trained technicians. Sooner or later they would have come up with something. It was unlikely that someone could kill her and put her in my closet without leaving some important clue.

Slowly I began to realize that while I had thought that I was being sane, logical and efficient, I had actually been in a state of emotional shock. I hadn't been thinking well at all. I had stupidly managed to destroy any possible clue. I had gotten myself out of a jam—maybe. And had given the actual murderer a priceless bonus. When the body was found, the murderer might very well be able to prove that he couldn't possibly have carted it twenty-five miles north into the woods. He was going to be highly pleased with my cooperation. Little by little the full knowledge of my own stupidity came to me. I had reacted from fright. Maybe what I had done took me out of the play, and maybe it didn't. If it didn't take me out, if I had made some mistake, overlooked something, I had destroyed whatever would prove my own innocence.

If I had made a mistake, it was going to be final. "Ladies and gentlemen of the jury, the State intends to prove that the defendant, Clinton Sewell, did murder the deceased, Mary Olan, and hide her body in the closet in the bedroom of his apartment until the following noon when, using the pretext of taking trash to the city dump, he placed her body, wrapped in a tarpaulin, in the trunk compartment of his car and took it to a deserted spot in the hills and left it there. The State intends to prove that subsequent to disposing of the body in the aforesaid manner, Sewell did continue on up to Smith Lake and pretended that he expected the deceased to join him there."

They could make me look like a monster. I felt cold all over. And then I thought of something that made me even colder. Assume the police, following up the question of motive, got close to the actual murderer. He knows what he did with the body. He would know by inference what I had done with the body. It would be the easiest thing in the world for him to steer them back toward me. A little lie here and there, maybe a lie about what the deceased had told him—not admissible as evidence, but enough to put them on my trail. "Why yes, Mary told me that Sewell was getting out of hand. She said he'd tried to choke her and then claimed it was just a joke. She said she was a little scared and wasn't going out with him again after that Saturday night."

I ordered some more hot coffee. I'd been very clever. Just as clever as a man I remembered back in the Fall River plant the first year I had worked for C.P.P. He operated a steam hammer in the forge shop. The hammer wouldn't come down. So he leaned in over the bed and looked up at it, curious no doubt as to why it wouldn't come down, and wiggled the lever. It came down that time.

I began to get into such a panic that I even considered going back and retrieving the tarp and the body, taking it home, replacing the red belt and making my belated phone call. After the second time around, I discarded that idea. I'd put myself in this situation. The only thing I could do was carry on. And pray. Pray I hadn't slipped.

The second cup was too hot to drink. I put it down. There was a lingering soreness in my head. It was unlike any headache I had ever had. A new thought shocked me. Maybe the headache indicated something. Maybe it indicated that I was the one who had done it. Maybe she had come back to the apartment. From what I knew of her, such an impulse wouldn't be entirely alien to her. And I had . . .

No, damn it. The mind is a strange thing, but not that strange. At least mine wasn't. If the police had found her in my closet, they could have determined a few things quickly. If she had been attacked, if she had any skin under her sharp fingernails. I remembered reading that they could type fragments of skin, like blood.

I was getting too restless to stay there. And it occurred to me that I didn't want to spend too much time in transit between the apartment and Smith Lake. I asked for some water, dumped some in the coffee, finished the coffee and left.

The Olan place at Smith Lake was built back in the days when, if you wanted a place at a lake you built a house. None of this camp nonsense. It was stone, two stories and an attic, but the ceilings on both floors were so high the house looked three stories high. Three or maybe even four generations of kids living up the summers had beaten its original grandeur into a condition of scarred comfort. The other places on the lake were surrounded by woods and brush. The Olan land was cleared and seeded. It sat on a wide expanse of green that sloped down toward the lake shore and the boat houses. Up near the road was the horse barn and garages. I had been there twice before, and met all the clan. During the summer there is a staff of four. An ancient iron Swedish lady called Mrs. Johannsen does the cooking. Her round shy maiden lady of a daughter, called Ruth, does the cleaning and helps in the kitchen. They both come out from the Pryor house in town, as does John Fidd, a knobbly, sour man who brings up three or four saddle horses from the Pryor farm and reluctantly takes care of the grounds, obviously considering yard work beneath him. The remaining staff member, Nels Yeagger, is a massive, amiable young brute who is hired locally—has been for the past three summers—to take care of the boats and do odd jobs.

With this complete staff, the Olans and the Pryors come and go as they please. With the bedrooms in the big house, and the bunk rooms on the second floor of each boat house, quite a crowd can be accommodated. People ask their own friends and stick together, so that it is entirely possible to spend a day there without even meeting some of the other guests. The two times I had been there it had reminded me more than anything else of an old small private club, so long established that there are special customs and even a special language. Nobody makes any effort to entertain you. Unless you're willing to stir around, you can be lonesome.

I counted eight other cars up by the horse barn when I parked. I took my swimming trunks out of the glove compartment and went down to the house. Mary's younger brother was in the living room. He's a thin pale boy with heavy black hair that starts about an inch above his eyebrows. He's a remote, terribly dignified boy, and handles himself with a certain style. He was wearing a black turtleneck sweater and white shorts, and he was sitting staring at a big chessboard on which a game was apparently in progress. As I looked at him he moved a piece and made a notation in a notebook.

When I walked in he looked up and said, "Hello . . . uh . . . Clint."

"What are you doing?"

He looked amused. "Do you want me to tell you?"

"Go ahead. Just for kicks."

"I'm making a prepared variation involving the second move of the king's bishop in the Nimzoindian Defense. I hope to use it in a tournament next month in New York, right after school lets out."

"You figure these things out ahead?"

He gave me a lofty, patient look. *"All* tournaments are won these days with prepared variations of one kind or another."

"Are you pretty good, John?"

"After this tournament, if I do as well as I hope, I'll be the fifth ranking player in the country." He grinned suddenly. "You don't give a damn about this, so why ask?" For that instant he looked so much like Mary that it nearly broke my heart.

"Is Mary around?"

"Didn't you hear? Aunt Myrna is spinning. Little Mary

didn't come home at all last night. She and Uncle Willy are down in town heckling the police."

"I heard about that. The police came to see me this morning because I was out with her last night. I figured she'd be here by now."

"She'll turn up. She always has. But Aunt Myrna always worries. Mary's no child, she's twenty-six. I'm no child either, but try and convince Aunt Myrna." Before I was out of the room he was back in his special two-dimensional world, engrossed in the cruel slant of the bishops, the hungry eccentric leap of the knights.

I walked on down to the beach, to the stretch of sand between the two boat houses. There were a lot of people there, most of them familiar to me. I waved to a few, went to the men's bunk room and changed. Then I started circulating on the beach, sitting on my heels to talk to various groups. They were casually interested in the fact that Mary was missing. It was a mild game to try to guess what had happened to her—what she had taken it into her head to do.

I saw that the three girl children of Willy and Myrna Pryor were there. They were, of course, Mary's first cousins. They are aged fifteen, sixteen and seventeen. They are brown and husky and pretty, with crisp brown hair. Due to Willy's absence in town, they were considerably more relaxed with their three male guests than I had seen them on other occasions. Their swim suits were of the ultra-conservative cut (Willy's idea, probably), but one of them was using the small of her boyfriend's back as a pillow. Another girl provided a pillow for her escort in the form of a round brown thigh. The third pair had their heads together, whispering. The girls are called Jigger, Dusty and Skeeter—but I do not know which is which. They make me feel very very old.

I had seen some of the other guests at the club last night and they knew I had been out with Mary, so I had to tell my story several times, always careful not to deviate from the one I had given the two officers who woke me up. I kept thinking of the silent body I had left in the woods.

I took a short swim and came back to the beach. Somebody gave me a can of cold beer. I was talking to a dainty blonde who seemed to be making a sun-dazed pass at me when I saw Dodd walking toward the beach, obviously looking for someone. He saw me and headed for me, smiling and waving at friends as he passed them.

He is my boss. He's as tall as I am, but thirty pounds heavier. The extra weight is not concentrated in any one place—it is all over him in an even layer, blurring his outline. His brown-blond hair is wavy, worn just a shade too long. Except for his mouth, his features are good, and his color is high. His mouth is a bit small, so that in anger his expression becomes a bit pinched and womanish. He has friendly, hearty mannerisms. He is almost a nice guy. That was what made it so rough when he reported—to find out he was almost a nice guy.

His predecessor, my previous boss, had been the best there is.

chapter 3

I have been with Consolidated Pneumatic Products, Incorporated, for five years. It is one of the big ones. You hear more about G.E. and General Motors because they have consumer lines and keep the name in front of the public. C.P.P. sells strictly to industry. You find the two page ads in the technical journals. There are sixteen plants, of which the Warren Tube and Cylinder Division is one of the smaller ones.

I started out in Fall River, was moved next to Buffalo, and then out to Warren a year ago. C.P.P. believes in keeping all managerial talent on the jump. Three years in any one place is about as long as you can expect. It is smart policy. It makes your executive talent in all echelons interchangeable and broadens your men. It facilitates standard management methods and procedures. And when a boy graduates from the gypsies to top management he will know quite a few of the plants intimately, and know personally a great many men in the field.

So many of the big corporations have adopted this plan that it has developed a whole new class of people in this country, people without roots. Or, perhaps, people with a different kind of roots. There are thousands upon thousands of us—the married couples filling up places like Park Forest, Illinois, like the two Levittowns, like Parkmerced in San Francisco, and Drexelbrook in Philadelphia. And, of course, like Warren's smaller version, Brookways. It is the new management caste, and what it will eventually turn into, nobody knows. Joe Engineer and his wife move out of Parkmerced and into Park Forest two thousand miles away. The first day they are there they can start playing do-you-know with their neighbors. Get the latest word. Wilsie quit and went with Reynolds Metals. Dupont sent Kingley back to the business school. The Bowens have three kids now. They live in the big developments, work on community committees, set up sitter banks and draw on each other's time; live with a minimum of privacy and a maximum of borrowing of gadgets, party glasses and utensils.

As a bachelor, I have not yet gotten into the community living aspects of this gypsy existence. Doubtless it will happen to me one day. A married man seems to have better promotion chances with top management.

I reported to the Warren plant, to Harvey Wills, the plant manager, on a rainy April day thirteen months ago, as the new assistant production manager. I was flushed with brand new promotion and raise, though apprehensive about the personnel, even though Tory Wylan, my personal spy and friend in the home offices in New York had told me it was a good group.

It turned out to be fine. Ray Walt was a sweetheart. He gave me my head and we worked well together. Ray was transferred in January, and Dodd Raymond came in. Before Ray left he told me he'd tried to get me promoted to his job, but the home office and Harvey Wills both thought I was a little too green for it. He told me, though he didn't have to, to keep my guard high with Dodd Raymond. He said Raymond was smart and ambitious, and had the reputation of always having a fall guy handy when something went sour. I thanked him.

Harvey Wills called me up to his office the day Dodd arrived, both to meet him and to give him the guided tour. Dodd shook hands the right way, said the right things, dressed the right way, and let me call him Mr. Raymond just one time. I wondered if Ray had been wrong.

But a week after Dodd reported I had a personal letter from Tory Wylan. He confirmed what Ray had told me. He filled in the details of some raw situations Dodd had been mixed up in. He'd trampled some good men and he'd come out on top. Tory wrote that Dodd had some of the top management fooled. The proof was in the fact that Dodd had been able to get a transfer to his own home town—a thing that was strictly against C.P.P. policy.

So, had I not been forewarned, maybe I would have thought Dodd a nice guy. He knew the business and stayed out of my hair. I protected myself by starting a work journal, dictating into it all orders he gave me.

After he and his wife got settled he had me to their place for drinks and dinner, with his wife and his mother. That was the beginning. That's how I started to get mixed up in the lives of Dodd and Nancy Raymond. Were it not for Dodd, and his being a home town boy with a considerable social pedigree, I would never have gotten to meet Mary Olan, much less endure the motel fiasco and later find her body in my closet. Dodd threw me and Mary Olan together, because he needed a cat's paw.

He had spotted me on the beach and he came on over. In grey suit and necktie he looked far too dressed up for Smith Lake.

"Hello, Marilyn, Clint. Certainly is a beautiful day up here. Getting hot as hell in town. Clint, can I talk to you a minute?"

It had more of a heavy-boss flavor than I liked, but I excused myself and walked over near the boat house with him.

"What's up?"

"There's nothing new about Mary. I dropped Nancy off at Mother's camp. Clint, I'm really worried about her. This isn't like her. She invited most of these people here."

"They seem to be doing fine."

"Did she act all right when she dropped you off?"

"She was fine and dandy, Dodd. Just like I told the police you sicked on me."

"Don't be like that, boy! Hell, they asked me. I had to tell them."

"You're pretty jittery."

"Mary is one of my best friends. You know that."

Sure. One of his best friends. And he thought he was pulling the wool over Nancy's eyes in fixing it up so Mary would date me and the four of us could make a nice jolly foursome. But I knew, as he didn't know, that he wasn't fooling Nancy a damn bit. Mary, in her own special way, had been making a fool out of Dodd Raymond. Maybe she actually wanted him. Or maybe she had been merely getting even for his unthinkable disloyalty in marrying a stranger without asking her permission first. I hadn't been able to figure out which it was. I only knew that he wanted Mary Olan and that I had been a handy device to keep her within range. Mary had been seven years younger than Dodd. But they had known each other well before he had moved away from Warren. How well I could only guess.

"How is Nancy taking it?" I asked maliciously.

"She's upset too, naturally. But let's leave my wife out of it for the time being, shall we? You don't seem to give a damn about Mary, Clint."

"She'll turn up," I said.

"When you get dressed why don't you drive over to the camp? Mother will be pleased to see you. We can have a few drinks and talk this thing over."

I said I would. It would be pleasant to see Nancy, at least. When the sun had dried me I said goodby to Marilyn, who pouted at me for leaving. There was no need to say goodby to anyone else.

I drove down the lake shore road to the sign which said, in copper and stained wood, RAYMOND. Each year Dodd's mother moved up to the small, comfortable camp at the lake with her nurse as soon as the weather was warm enough, leaving, this summer, the big house in town for Dodd and Nancy rather than closing it up. I imagined that it was a relief to Nancy to have the house to herself. Mrs. Raymond was an imposing, stone-faced, white-haired woman in her sixties, confined by arthritis to a wheelchair. She had positive opinions, and achieved emphasis through repetition. In her scale of values the fact that I worked for Dodd put me on almost the same social footing as the brawny Irish nurse who lifted her in and out of her wheelchair.

I parked the car in the drive and went around to the front where I knew they'd be. The shoreline is steep at that place. There is a patio on the lake side, and steep wooden steps that go down to the shallow beach. Dodd had changed to bright yellow shorts, and he had a can of beer in his hand. Mrs. Raymond sat in her wheelchair in the shade of a big beach umbrella. Nancy was stretched out on a padded chaise longue with wheelbarrow handles and wooden wheels. Her smile was what I had come to see.

"Well, young man," Mrs. Raymond said, "I suppose they're all running around in mad circles up at the Pryors' now that it's too late."

The final two words gave me a jolt. "Too late, Mrs. Raymond?"

"Of course it's too late. White slavers."

"Please, Mother," Dodd said. "Can I get you a beer, Clint?" I nodded.

"White slavers," Mrs. Raymond said firmly. "You don't hear much about them. They keep it out of the papers. You wait and see. Even if they didn't get her this time, they'll get her next time. You wait and see."

Dodd came back out of the kitchen and handed me a cold beer. "Mother has them crouched behind every bush."

"You can make it sound ridiculous all you want. You can jeer at me. But did they ever find the Cornwall girl? Did they? Did they ever find the slightest trace of her?

No, and they never will. After what they do to them
they're ashamed to come home," she said darkly.

"Maybe she just decided to go on a trip or something," Nancy said.

"Ha!" said Mrs. Raymond. Nancy's opinions always
got a similar response. I suspected that Mrs. Raymond
resented Nancy not only because she had married an
only son, but because after some six years of marriage
Nancy had yet to come up with a grandchild for her.

Nancy was wearing a figured grey sunsuit thing, with
a sort of skirt effect. She stretched and said, "Gosh, the
sun is making me sleepy. Anybody want to walk on the
beach?" Her glance swept across me meaningfully and I
rose to the hook.

"I'd just as soon."

"You two go ahead," Dodd said casually. A bit too
casually, I thought.

We went down the steep wooden stairs, Nancy first.
She is my favorite candybox blonde. Small perfect delicate features, silky floating hair. She has a thin little-
girl voice with overtones of a lisp cured long ago. How-
ever, there is a level honesty and intelligence in her blue
eyes that keeps her from being insipid. Her figure is
flawed, if you can consider it a flaw. I have no doubt
that she does, because her clothes, even the sunsuit, are
styled to de-emphasize the flaw. She is very long-waisted.
Her torso, discernible through any clothing, is long, ripe,
muscular, perfectly formed. You see such torsos carved
in old marble a lot oftener than you see them on people.
Were her legs in proportion Nancy would be six feet
tall. But the lovely torso rests on short heavy legs. They
are shapely, but they do not fit. Understand, it is not
something you see immediately. After you see her a few
times you begin to realize that though she is lush indeed,
the proportions are subtly off. Then you see why. Her
hips are too far from her head, and too close to the
ground.

We walked to a pine log a hundred yards up the beach.

"He's pretty upset," she said.

"Yes."

"Clint, do you have any remote idea what could have happened?"

"Not the slightest."

"It's damned funny. I . . . I hope she never comes back." Nancy said that shyly. We could not talk together of Mary Olan without constraint. She became shy when she remembered the way she had talked the second time we had all gone out as a foursome. Sober, Nancy would not have confided in me—I had been a stranger.

Dodd had set up the first double date. There had been undercurrents of tension that I didn't understand. Mary and Dodd would begin to close Nancy and me out of the conversation by talking of old friends during the old days in Warren. Then they would remember their manners. Mary's attitude toward me had been casual and friendly, but to Nancy she was patronizing. Nancy had kept her claws unsheathed just enough so they showed. I chalked that up to the normal stress you would expect between wife and old gal friend. I even assumed that Dodd had decided, since he was going to stay in Warren for some time, that the best way to smooth things out was to throw wife and old gal together and rub the edges off.

For my part, I was pleased. My social contacts in Warren were limited. The guys on my same level in the firm were out there in Brookways, well wifed and bairned. They had me out a few times for dinner. During the evening people would be drifting in and out, and some of them were lovely ladies. But each of the lovely ladies had a husband who just happened to be somewhere else that evening, and a place like Brookways—even if you had the inclination, which I most certainly haven't—is no place to make passes amid the married set. Compared to Brookways, a fishbowl is a mountain retreat.

There were, of course, the gals in the office. But C.P.P. regards such goings on with a paternalistic frown.

Warren is a tight community. I was part of the new influx of postwar population, and a professional transient at that. The old part of town drew its skirts tightly around itself, talked about the dreadful habits of the "new element," and quietly raised its standard of living with the money we were bringing in. So I had battered myself into apathy with workouts at the Y, with sheafs of work I brought home from the office, with library books that I had never gotten around to reading before. When restlessness got its sharp little fangs into me, I'd roam the Saturday bars. That is a forlorn pursuit, eyeing the tight-skirt little drabs in the neighborhood joints, or the enameled Vogue-like birds of prey in the dollar-a-cocktail lounges, nursing their pale poison during the five o'clock ritual of appraisal and rejection. The jukes hammer your head and your need is a sickness to be assuaged only by predictable shame.

During my five transient years I had come to learn that the more complex the civilization grows, the more violent are the effects of loneliness. I had learned why C.P.P., G.E., Dupont, Alcoa, Ford, General Motors, Kodak and all the rest of them wanted us safely married. Still, there were a lot of us still single, minds honed keen by Sheffield, Towne, Stanford, Harvard Business, M.I.T., and by day we made things run and move and grow. But by night we paced the neon sidewalks where nylon whispers on hips and ankles, and lipstick shows black when the light overhead is red.

A few times I had reached the point where the act of marriage became a goal in itself, apart from any specific woman. Marriage to a faceless being who was nevertheless all too vivid from the neck down, who by warmth and closeness would still the gnaw of the blood.

Thus I was grateful to Dodd for being willing and able to give me this chance to enter a world previously denied me. Mary Olan opened a door and the city changed. Sewell, through Dodd, sponsored by Olan, became acceptable. They saw to their indubitable surprise that I unerringly chose the correct fork, that my shoulders were unpadded, that I tied my own bow tie, that I could carry on a conversation that had absolutely nothing to do with helical gears, cutter grinders and industrial abrasives. I soon learned that the old line families thought Dodd's career with C.P.P. rather daring and eccentric. With law, medicine and banking open to him, he had become a technical man. Works down at one of those new plants beyond the river, doing God knows what. It's really charming that he could arrange to be sent back home. They ship them around like cattle, you know. That little wife he found somewhere or other actually seems rather sweet. And it seemed so dreadfully obvious that he would marry the Olan girl. Much as I was amused and irritated by the attitude of Old Warren, I was sophomorically delighted to become known and accepted.

It was on my second date with Mary Olan that Nancy Raymond, inhibitions liquidated, bared her distressed soul. A woman with a top sergeant voice had phoned me at the office and given me my orders regarding a party she was giving at the Locust Ridge Club. I checked with Dodd and he said it had been his suggestion. I was to pick up Mary and the four of us could go together. When I phoned Mary I found out that she had been given her orders too.

It was an April Saturday night, a cocktail party for about forty in a private room at the club, then dinner and dancing. My appearance with Mary Olan made it essential that each one of the other guests meet me, categorize me and put me on a mental list for future parties should I pass inspection.

Nancy looked charming in a dinner dress that was exactly the right color and cut for her—a slate blue that enhanced her eyes and emphasized the incredibly fine texture of her skin. After I had been punted from group to group with rugby precision, I found myself in a restful corner with Nancy.

"The man who mixed these martinis belongs at White Sands," I said.

Nancy was looking beyond me at Dodd, standing with Mary Olan in a group of eight. Mary, laughing heartily, had taken Dodd's arm.

"Skoal," Nancy said and thumped two-thirds of a cocktail down her throat in two gulps and handed me her glass. "Please, mister."

I brought her a new one. She took half of it, said, "To White Sands," and downed the second half.

"Easy, my lady. These can be poison."

"Hah! Fade me again, Clint boy."

"I will not be a party to self-destruction, Nance."

"I'll get it my own self."

"Okay, okay." It was not happy to watch. I wondered if our Nancy were a lush. I decided no. Female lushes carry the mark on them. Their faces coarsen, their features thicken, they grow fur on the larynx. So it had to be the Mary Olan situation, and an intensification of the strain I had noticed on the first date.

The four of us ate at a table for six with another couple. I was between Nancy and a hollow-eyed brunette with a staccato bray of a laugh which made her husband, across the table, wince visibly each time she tinkled the chandeliers with it. Nancy had somehow managed to get a double martini at the table. When Dodd reached over for it, she wrapped her hand around it. She had reached the glazed state, monosyllabic, practically inert. After too many awkward holes in the conversation, Mary Olan began to carry the ball. She did it well, too. Conversation bounced and pranced, passing back and forth in front of the dead eyes of Nancy Raymond. Mary kept hauling me in by the heels, but I still found time to whisper to Nancy that she should eat something. Her great slab of rare roast beef arrived and was removed untouched.

We were on coffee when she stood up abruptly. The conversation stopped and Dodd started to stand up too.

"Not you," she said to him with great clarity. "Have to walk. With Clint."

He gave a little nod and I went off with Nancy. She walked with rigid dignity until we were outside and then clung tightly to my arm. There had been a misty rain earlier. The stars were covered and the grass was wet. We could see by the light from the club.

"Special service," she said. "Walking drunk ladies."

"Where do we walk?"

"Round and around. Hooo. Dizzy as a bee."

We walked in silence back and forth across the wide grounds near the tennis courts. She kept lifting her head high and breathing deeply. We must have walked for fifteen minutes and then she said, "Sit down now. Over there."

We went over to some benches beside the tennis courts. In the faint light the nets had a forlorn sag, the asphalt courts gleamed wetly. I used my handkerchief to wipe the dampness from a bench. We sat down and I lit our cigarettes.

"Clint, you ever try to . . . to match yourself against a great tradegy, tradegy . . . hell, tragedy."

"Can't say that I have."

"That Olan bitch. Her mother went crazy. Murdered her father. Dodd told me all about it when we were married. He wanted to marry her. No she says. Can't do. Insanity. Very tragic. I ask Dodd if he still loves her. No, no, no. Kid stuff. All over. Sure. Loves me. Just me. We're fine. Good marriage, Clint. It was. Then he starts wondering if he can get back here. Mother all crippled up. Lots of old friends. Me, damn fool me, I say why not. So a year ago he starts working angles. Pulls strings. Real careful. Back we come. Warren! I hate it. Oh, how I hate it. You see, she's here. And it isn't dead. It never was. Not with her and not with him. Oh, I got the picture. She won't play. She won't sneak. Very noble. He wants to see her, it's got to be right out in a open. Like this. Where she can work on him. Make me look bad. Pat the little wife on the head. Take him back just so she can show her muscles. Lots of money but a cheap bitch anyway, you know?"

"I don't think it's like that."

"Oh you don't! What do you know anyway? You're the patsy. You don't take her out. You just make her handy so she can work on him. And I can't do a damn thing. I can't say we don't go out with you two. That makes me look worse even. I have to stand still for it. I have to just wait and watch everything blow up. Good sport. Good old Nancy. Fine! Clint, you could fix it. If only she'd just . . . If you could make her . . . No, I can't say that. Won't say that. Won't ask you to do anything like that."

"Want to walk some more?"

"It was so wonderful. We had our kind of friends. Everywhere we went. Not like these people. They act like his job stinks. Like it's a . . . a hobby. These aren't my kind of people. You know what? He won't let me tell anybody here. It was okay to tell it other places where we lived. Big joke. We could laugh. Here he hasn't got any sense of humor. Know how I met him? Want to bust laughing? I cleaned his teeth. Dental hygienist. Kept coming back to get his teeth cleaned. Had the cleanest teeth in the country. Had to marry him before I wore 'em right down to the gums. Other places we could tell that. Not here. Here it would be like dirt. Like I'm something to be ashamed of. Gee, it isn't something you can just *do*. You have to study for it. I studied hard. I was good. What's wrong with that?"

She sounded so lost I wanted to take her in my arms. I wanted to anyway—even drunk she was a desirable woman. And I wanted to smack Dodd Raymond right in the nose. There wasn't a damn thing I could say to her.

She stood up suddenly and said in an awed voice, "I'm going to be sick."

We went over to some bushes. I held her and held her

head as she was wrenchingly ill. Then I went up to the men's room at the club and got a wet towel and a dry towel and took them back down to her. She bathed her face and then used the towels on the spattered front of her dress. As she bent over, working on her dress, she said, "How awful, Clint. How perfectly awful."

"It happens to the carefullest."

"I wasn't very careful. You're sweet, Clint."

"Friend of the family."

"Would you do me one more thing?"

"Sure."

"Drive me home. Don't tell Dodd you're doing it. Tell him when you get back. If you tell him now he'll insist on taking me home. He won't say anything later but he'll have that damn patient look that will mean I spoiled the party. Added to everything else, of course. Do you mind?"

"No. Want to leave now?"

"Please."

I drove her to the Raymond home. It was a high-shouldered job, mansard roof, iron fence, in a neighborhood that was decaying in slow genteel fashion, preparing its soul for the inevitable invasion of funeral parlor, supermarket and masseuse. The big house was dark.

"We moved Mother Raymond up to the place at the lake early this afternoon," she explained. "I wouldn't dare come home alone if she was here. She said it was earlier than usual for her. Then she sighed and she said it would be nice for us two young people to be alone. And she sighed again and said she hoped it wouldn't be so damp at the lake this time of year, and so cold that it would hurt her arthritis. Sigh, sigh, sigh. Damn it all!"

I walked her up to the door and she handed me the key. I opened the big door and it creaked as it swung back. She reached inside and found a switch that turned on the light in the big narrow gloomy hallway.

"Clint, I talked too much. I talked an awful lot too much."

"I can't remember a darn word, somehow."

"Can I tell you you're a nice guy?"

"Sure."

"You're a nice guy. What I said is between us. I'm unhappy here and I drank too much and I'm ashamed of myself. This isn't my house and it doesn't seem like my husband any more and I became a fool tonight. I won't do it again. That isn't the way to fight this thing. That's the way to hand him to her on a platter, with an apple and cloves. I'll do better."

"I know you will, Nancy. Temporary lapse. Maybe overdue."

She smiled. "If I wasn't so messy, I'd like to be kissed."

I put my hands on her shoulders and kissed her forehead. "That do?"

"It does fine, Clint. Goodnight . . . and thanks."

I drove back to the club. The dancing had started. The five piece orchestra sounded like an awkward fusion of Meyer Davis and Bobby Hackett. Every other number was mechanical Latin, gourds and all. Dodd wasn't on the floor. I tracked him down over in the men's bar. He was talking down at a man who looked like a bald Pekingese. When I caught his eye he wound up the conversation and came over to me, glass in hand.

"Where's Nancy?"

"She didn't feel good. She had me take her home."

"Why didn't you tell me? I could have taken her home."

"She wanted it that way."

"I've never seen her do that before. I can't understand what got into her." He glanced at me sideways, suspicion shining in his eyes.

I made a noncommittal sound. It was no time for a brand new friend of the family to tell husband he knew what was wrong with wife.

"Did she tell you what was eating on her?"

"No. Is something?"

"There must be, for her to act like this. My God, she

knows how this town is. They'll clack for a week. I suppose I ought to get on home. Wait a minute, we all
came in your car. Well, I can get a taxi."

"She sounded as if she'd like it better if you stayed,
Dodd. She said she didn't want to spoil your evening."

"Any more than she already has." He finished his
drink, reached over and set the empty glass on the bar.
"I might as well hang around, I guess. Buy you a drink,
Clint?"

"Not right now, thanks."

He put his hand on my shoulder, gave me a couple
of squeezes. I was born with a catlike aversion to such
stray gestures. I merely endure them, hoping my expression doesn't give away my distaste. Besides, there was
something forced about the way he did it. He looked at
me intently. "Clint, I've never had a chance to tell you
how damn well much it means to me to come out here
and find a guy like you to help carry the ball. I mean
that."

"Well, thanks, Dodd."

"You know what you can get sometimes in this outfit. A politico. An oily switch artist. Hell, I know where
you stand."

He took his hand off my shoulder, made a fist out of
it and punched me lightly in the arm. "We're both going
places in this outfit, boy."

I told him I hoped so and watched his broad back
as he went off toward the festivities. It was obvious that
he had just enough quasi-feminine perception to sense
that Nancy had somehow acquired an ally; how much
else she might have in me he couldn't tell. He wanted
to pour a little water on the flame. Deciding that wouldn't
do, he had built a back fire. I cannot say that it was in-
effective—mellow words from the boss are always wel-
come. And he was almost a nice guy.

Between eleven and twelve the party was in overdrive.
Every time I saw Mary she was with Dodd. A junior
miss who took considerable pride in the gaudy details of

the recent escapade that had gotten her tossed out of Sweet Briar on her pretty tail, had taken me over and kept bruising my morale by frequent references to how much "older men" appealed to her.

She steered me, not too unwillingly, out into the darkness. But when I came to kiss her she sagged softly against me, a boneless, gasping, wide-mouthed horror. I have no idea where and how such a response happened to become fashionable among the younger set. Maybe they think it sets a mood of sweet surrender. You reach for a firm-boned young morsel and she falls into suet. I pushed her away and eased her back into the bright lights.

After the first cut-in I moved back out into the shrubbery alone. The clouds had thinned and a moon cruised blandly through the ragged edges. Music thudded out across the somber fairways. I fingered an empty cigarette package and remembered the half carton in the glove compartment. I walked across the grass toward the parking lot.

I was close enough to the car to touch it when I heard Mary Olan's voice coming from inside the car. Her tone was lazy, taunting. "My dear, you aren't on the basis where all you have to do is whistle. So I won't take your key. Any time I go back there—if I ever do go back there—you'll damn well be there waiting for me, not I for you. This isn't Back Street, sweets."

Dodd's heavy voice said, "This double-dating is childish."

"Is it? I know what you want. You want me waiting there for you any time you happen to take a notion. You don't want me to go out at all. I happen to like this arrangement. Clint is sweet. Wasn't he sweet with your plotzed Nancy?"

"Are you falling for him? Damn it, if I find out you've let him get to you, I'll get him shipped so far away from here he'll . . ."

"Jealous, darling?" she drawled.

"Why don't you just take the key and then . . ."

"You want one cake to eat, one to look at and one in the cupboard. No thanks. I might decide never to pay you another visit there."

"Mary, listen to me . . ."

"You listen to me. You're boring me. That wasn't in the agreement. I'll continue to go out with Clint. You'll continue to come along too, with Nancy. It's a cozy arrangement. . . . And I'm getting sick of sitting here like a college girl on a date."

"But tonight Clint took her home and we could . . ."

"We could but we won't, dear. Not tonight. Face it like a brave little man."

I had stood there and listened. And learned a great deal. It was a situation that smelled faintly of mental illness.

"But Mary . . ."

"And, darling, I didn't like that phrase 'get to me.' People don't 'get to me.' I get to people. Now if you'd take that slightly clumsy hand off my breast . . ."

I moved back fast as the door latch clicked. She got out of the car quickly. She'd have seen me if she'd turned my way, but she headed off, heels punching the gravel, toward the front door of the club. I was back in better cover when Dodd got out and lighted a cigarette. I watched him take three long draws, then snap it away toward the wet grass. He followed her slowly. When I got my cigarettes the interior of the car was heavy with the perfume she used, a musky, offbeat scent.

When I drove them home I dropped Dodd off first. Mary Olan didn't move over next to the door after he got out. She stayed pleasantly and encouragingly close to me, the side of her leg touching mine. I took her out to the Pryor place where I had picked her up. Though a lot of the old line families have stayed down in the shady quiet streets of town, a few, such as Willy Pryor, have built out in the country. It has a stone wall, a bronze sign, a quarter mile of curving drive before you get to it. Probably the outmoded term for it would be a machine for living. You know the type—all dramatics. Dramatic window walls, dramatic bare walls, dramatic vistas. Two floodlighted pieces of statuary—one all sheet aluminum and the other a grey stone woman with spider limbs and great holes right through her where breasts should have been. The architects do fine, they can really set up a place. The only trouble is that no one has been similarly occupied redesigning people. Such machines cannot sit in sterile functional perfection. We people have to move in—bringing, of course, our unmodified belch, our unreconstructed dandruff, our enlarged pores and our sweaty love.

I parked and Mary made no move toward the door handle, so I gathered her in and kissed her. She hesitated for a stilted second and then baked the enamel on my teeth. She was no pulpy junior miss. She brought to the task at hand a nice interplay of musculature, a crowding enthusiasm, and the durability and implacability of a Marciano. She stopped all clocks except the one in the blood, so that on terminus, I was dimly startled to find myself merely sitting in my own automobile.

"You're an agreeable monster, Sewell," she said softly.

"Likewise."

"You should get a bonus for overtime."

"A truly obscure remark," I said, pretending young innocence.

"Would, Sewell, that I were a touch more charitable and I would make of myself a suitable bonus, because I suspect you are a nice guy who deserves a better deal than you are getting."

"Tonight is my night to be told I'm a nice guy. How do I go about arousing your charitable instincts, lady?"

She permitted a second flanking operation. During same I investigated traditionally, hopefully, a breast warm and classic. She rebanked her fires and extricated lips and breast, putting a cold foot of distance betwixt us.

"No sale, Sewell."

"Anything my best friends have neglected to tell me?"

"Nope. You are a fine crew-cut, long-limbed specimen of young American manhood, my dear."

"They why?"

"Don't ask it with a pout. I guess it is because you are what you are. For a man to intrigue me he must have a wide streak of son-of-a-bitch."

"I can work on that."

"Hardly."

"Could you force yourself?"

She reached a quick hand and knuckled the top of my head. "That would be pure charity, sweets, and you have too much pride for that, don't you?"

"And the next line is let us be good friends."

"Seriously, I'd like that, Clint. I need a good friend."

I sighed with resignation. "Okay, what do you want to do with your good friend on the morrow."

"Wouldst go to church with me, sir?"

It was quite the last thing I expected. "Yes. Of course."

"Pick me up here at twenty of eleven then."

I walked her to her door. She smiled up at me. "You *are* sweet."

"Then pat me on the head, damn it."

"Temper, temper! Kiss goodnight."

As that kiss ended I took revenge with my long right arm. She yelped and took a cut at me and missed. As I drove home I knew that if she had a full-length mirror and looked back down over her shoulder within the next ten minutes, she could admire a nice distinct hand print.

Looking back I can count over twenty dates with her, including the time at the motel and the last one on the night of Saturday, May fifteenth. But not including that last ride we took together, up into the hills. Date from which she would not return.

chapter 4

Nancy and I sat on the pine log. She smoked her cigarette and scratched at a punkie bite on her ankle. Ever since the night she had gotten drunk and told me her woes, we had talked frankly with each other, though she had retained an aura of shyness. I had not told her what I had learned that night. There was no point in it. Suspicions could hurt, but the actuality would be worse.

"I hope . . . I hope she never comes back," Nancy said.

I didn't say anything for too long and the words hung there between us until Nancy laughed mirthlessly. "I don't mean I hope anything bad has happened to her. Even to her. I just hope she's found some other fly to pull the wings off."

"She's impulsive," I said.

"Nice polite word. She's a harpy. She feeds on people. She has a nice built-in excuse—her insane mother. That's handy for her. No marriage, so she does as she pleases. Including going to bed with my husband."

"You aren't positive of that, though."

"Oh, I am, Clint. Entirely certain. I kidded myself for a long time. But you can't live with a man and not know. All the little false touches. That blandness, with all the guilt underneath. I know, Clint. I've known for a long time. It started back in February, a month after we arrived. She didn't waste any time, did she?"

"Don't try to laugh about it."

"Aren't I supposed to be gay about it? Isn't that so-

phisticated or something? Last night after we got home
we had a real scrap. He wouldn't admit it, of course. I
asked him about the things that are missing. His good
robe, some sports shirts, an extra pair of slippers—little
things like that. And a book of poems. Poems! My God,
can you imagine reading poems to a . . . a thing like
that? I asked him if it would ease his conscience any if
I took a lover. You know, continental style. Sauce for
the goose. At that he stormed out and didn't come back
until five this morning. Anyway, I wanted to talk to you,
Clint. I haven't told him or anybody else, but I'm going to leave him."

"Do you mean that?"

"I have some pride. I don't have to put up with this.
I can earn my own living. It hurts . . . hurts badly,
Clint, when someone tells you in that way that you
aren't enough for them. Enough woman."

"You want to be awfully sure, Nancy."

"I am sure. I've told you so much of my personal
life. Aren't you sick of it? Don't you want to know everything? The whole story? I have two small brown moles
right here on my left hip. Tomatoes give me a rash.
When I get emotionally upset, I get diarrhea. Nervous
colon they call it. I lost my virginity when I was sixteen
and had a job waiting on table at a summer . . ."

"Nancy!" Her voice had gone shrill and her face
was tense.

The tension went out of her. She put her head down
on her bare knees and said in a small voice, "I'm sorry,
Clint."

I touched the silky-fine blonde hair. "You've had it
rough. I don't blame you. But promise one thing. Think
about it for a week."

She sighed. "If you think I ought to."

"I do."

She sighed again. "Clint?"

"Yes, honey."

"Clint . . . do you want me?" Her voice was shy, far off.

I knew why she asked. I knew how careful I had to be. "Yes, of course. Any man would say yes. You're a special thing, Nancy."

"I'm not. But I'll . . . be special for you. When, Clint? And where?"

"I want you, but I don't think it would be smart. I think you still love the guy. He's hurt you badly. You want reassurance. You want to be wanted. And you want to hurt him back. I'm your friend, Nancy. I don't want to be caught in the middle of that sort of thing. Suppose he sees what a fool he's been, and you get back together. You'd always regret it. You've never done anything like that, have you?"

"No. I . . . I don't know what I want to do."

"Think for a week. Then we'll talk again. Okay?"

She lifted her head and looked at me. Her cheeks were wet. "Well you could anyway kiss me," she said almost fiercely.

No boats were near and they couldn't see us from the patio of the Raymond camp. I stood up, took her hand, pulled her up and kissed her. It lasted a long time. There was none of the quick flame of Mary. Nancy's lips were soft and warm and very sweet. But there was heat there, a slow burning—enough heat so I wondered how Dodd could be such an utter fool. We stepped apart and smiled at each other.

"I guess you're darn good for me," she said. "Like a sort of substitute conscience. I wish it was you I was in love with. It would be so much easier. And better."

"You're special, Nancy."

"Somebody has to think so. I guess we better get back now."

We climbed the steps. I was certain Mrs. Raymond checked me over quickly for signs of lipstick. Nancy had dabbed it off with a Kleenex. I said goodby as soon as I could and left.

I did not like driving by the entrance to the road where I had left Mary's body. Soon the night would come with small animals rustling through the shrubbery, with dew weighting the white skirt, misting the bare shoulders. There would be insect song and a riding moon. I wished I could have left her in a warm dry place. It couldn't matter to her, I knew, but it mattered to me. It didn't seem right.

I ate in town and it was dark when I turned into my drive. Mrs. Speers ran a window up and called to me. I braked the car, motor running.

"Has Mary Olan turned up yet, Mr. Sewell?" she asked.

"Not yet, Mrs. Speers."

"They must be getting very worried by now."

"I guess so."

"You won't forget my trash tomorrow, will you?"

"I'll remember it, Mrs. Speers."

"I guess you'll be going to bed right now, won't you?"

"How do you mean?"

She laughed. "Well, you know I heard you drive in at four, this morning."

"I was in by two, Mrs. Speers."

She laughed again. "You young folks, you lose track of time."

"I know it wasn't that late."

"Goodnight, Mr. Sewell." She closed the window.

Inside my apartment, I locked the door, turned on the lights, closed the blinds. It was good to be alone and in a locked place. I felt as though I would now be able to think clearly and consecutively. All day I had been playing a part. It had left no room for reflection. I felt as though my face ached from smiling. I had walked among the beach people, shaking hands with a hand that had carried the dead. It gave me an appreciation of that degree of iron control a murderer must have.

During the day I had learned two new facts: Dodd Raymond had been out of his house until five, and a car had driven into my driveway at four. I had no doubt but that the car at four had brought Mary to the place of her death. Probably Mrs. Speers, sleeping through my first arrival, hearing the arrival at four, turned over and went to sleep again and did not hear the car leave.

I had to think of Dodd as the suspect. I knew that he and Mary Olan had been having an affair. And I knew that Mary was cruel, taunting, ruthless—withholding herself on whim. I could imagine Dodd, infuriated beyond reason, striking her in anger, killing her. Maybe she had showed him the key I had given her, hinting at a reason for it which did not exist. Yes, he could have killed in sudden jealous anger. And, having killed in that way, knowing that I was a very sound sleeper, knowing the key was available, he would be capable of planting the body in my apartment. It would not be done out of malice toward me—though there would be some of that. It would be done as the most logical way of diverting suspicion.

Thus, had Mary died of a blow, or died with the mark of the strangler's hands on her throat, I would have had no doubt that it was Dodd. But the cause of death had been my red belt around her throat; the print of the weave had been in her flesh. And so she had been brought to my apartment to be killed there. And I could not see Dodd, ambitious and intelligent, premeditating something that could so easily have gone wrong. Had I constituted a serious threat to his career, it might be plausible. On the other hand ambition was a disease that could distort facts. Maybe he believed I was a threat to his career.

His worry about Mary had seemed genuine. Yet what Ray and Tory had told me seemed to indicate he was a good actor. Of course the affair itself had been a potential threat to his career. But ambitious men have been blinded by flesh before.

Like so many guessing games, this one came to a dead end. He could have, and he couldn't have. I could carry it right up to the final moment, and then my mind rebelled at the picture of Dodd bringing her into the apartment, selecting the belt, drawing the makeshift noose tightly around her throat.

When I took my pajamas from the closet, a drifting memory of her musky perfume remained there. I went to bed emotionally exhausted. In the faint light that came into the room I could see the open closet door, and I could imagine she was still there.

I slept and dreamed. I dreamed we all sat around a coffin. Mary sat up in the coffin, naked, the belt around her neck. Everyone looked at me. I explained that it was just a muscle reflex that made her sit up. She got out of the coffin and came to me. We danced. All the others kept time with a slow sad clapping of their hands, watching us as we danced. I kept whispering to Mary that she should get back into the coffin.

I looked down at her bare breast as we danced. Above the nipple was marked C.P.P. It was not tattooed, it was in black, in raised, shiny ornate letters, like the engraving on an expensive calling card. She said Dodd had done it, and the hideous mouth grinned. I said she had to get back into the coffin. She danced me to the coffin and I looked into it and saw why she could not. Nancy Raymond lay in the coffin, naked, her body gilded. On her body crouched a monstrous hairy spider with iridescent eyes. I awoke in cold sweating childhood terror and knew I had cried out because the echo of my cry seemed to be in the room. It was a long time before I slept again.

At eight-twenty-five the next morning, a grey gusty Monday, I parked with my front bumper under the little white sign that said MR. SEWELL. With such small conveniences are the souls of executives purchased. My office, along with the space assigned to Engineering and to Research, is on what you could call a mezzanine looking out over the main production floor. My secretary is in the room with me, along with filing cases for blueprints, a pair of drafting tables, my desk, sundry straight chairs. The office wall nearest the production area is duotherm glass from waist-height up. Beyond that wall is a railed catwalk that extends the length of the building, with a circular iron staircase at either end.

To get a piece of work out you need men, machines and materials at the right place at the right time. To facilitate this I have four production chasers, a production record clerk. I keep a beady eye on inventory, on quotas, on equipment maintenance, on absenteeism. With the system we have, it should run like watches. But it never does. If it isn't an industrial accident, then it's some storeroom monkey counting an empty box as being a hundred available items necessary for assembly. Next some setup man blunders and an automatic milling machine works busily all day turning out scrap. When things start to roll, a cancellation and change order comes in from on high. Then maintenance fumbles and we tear the gearing out of a turret lathe. You get behind and try to jolly the boys into doing a little back busting to catch up and the union steward comes around talking darkly about speedups. Then I have to go down on the floor with my time and motion study man and quack with the steward.

Half the time it is like working in a madhouse, and the rest of the time you are merely a one-armed juggler. I love it. There is always more than just keeping the thing running. Right now, coordinating with Engineering, I was in the middle of changing one of the lines, unbolting equipment, jackhammering places for new equipment, resetting conveyor lines. Sales, in New York, was hollering. I knew that once the new line was set and checked out, we'd have to go on two-shift operation.

I like to get there early. I like to stand out on the catwalk and look down for a few minutes at the silent waiting equipment. Its arrangement is an exercise in logic. All the beds and housings and turrets are cold grey, and all the moving parts are bright Chinese red. It is a good place to work. It is clean, air conditioned, well lighted. Labor relations are pretty good. C.P.P. is very mildly paternalistic, but not so much that the guy on the machine wishes they'd knock off the expensive fluff and put the difference in his envelope.

I took my morning look at the floor and then went into the small office next to mine where my records clerk works. I studied the big score board, made a mental note of the weak spots and went into my own office. It is air conditioned and sound-proofed, but with the door shut once the day gets going, the rumble of the floor can make you feel as though you're on an ocean liner. People go in and out my door all day long. Every time the door is opened the blast of pure noise, metal-cutting noise, is monstrous.

I had picked up a morning paper on the way to work, but I hadn't had a chance to do more than glance at a fat black headline—OLAN HEIRESS MISSING. I had expected newspaper coverage, but not so much. This went all the way across the top of page one, dwarfing a second headline about a Paris conference. I hadn't known Mary Olan was quite that important.

I spread the paper out on my desk to read the account. Warren has two papers, the morning *Ledger-Tribune* and the evening *Ledger-Record,* both owned by the same firm. Except on Monday, the morning paper is usually a warmed over version of the evening paper. They are excessively dull papers, full of editorial caution, unwilling to offend any local group. No particularly controversial syndicate columnist is ever used.

The subhead said, CAR FOUND ABANDONED NEAR HIGHLAND.

Mary Olan, twenty-six-year-old niece of Mr. and Mrs. Willis Pryor of this city, and heiress to the Rolph Olan estate, has been missing since late Saturday evening, and police state today that no trace of her has been found. A late model black convertible found yesterday near an abandoned farm south of Highlands was identified as belonging to the missing woman. A search of the surrounding area has been organized.

Miss Olan left the Pryor home on Saturday at noon, alone. She lunched at the Locust Ridge Club and, during the afternoon, played golf with Miss Neale Bettiger. She had taken other clothing to the club with her, and she dressed there and met friends for dinner and a club dance. She left the club after midnight, with the stated intention of returning to her home. It has been reported that Miss Olan did not seem disturbed or emotionally upset in any way.

Police have not ruled out the possibility of kidnaping, and a close watch is being kept on the Pryor home. They found no evidence of foul play in Miss Olan's automobile. She was last seen wearing a white skirt, a dark grey sleeveless blouse and high-heeled dark grey shoes. She is five feet four, brunette and weighs approximately a hundred and twenty pounds. Her eyes are grey.

Miss Olan is the granddaughter of Thomas Burke Olan who founded the Warren Citizens Bank and Trust Company, and Olan Tool and Die, which is now the Federated Tool Company, Inc.

Miss Olan was born in this city at the old Olan home on Prospect Street, now headquarters of the Heart of America Historical Association, which was given the property under the terms of Mr. Rolph Olan's will. Miss Olan was educated in private schools here and abroad, and has made her home here for the past four years.

It was typical tippy-toe Warren coverage. No mention of the family killing. No mention of Mary's abortive marriage and annulment. No hint of her mother's incurable illness. They'd even had her going home from the club at a more reasonable hour. I was glad that the police had apparently kept the name of her dinner dance companion to themselves. Otherwise I would have had a reporter or two hanging around. Or maybe not; perhaps the Warren papers thought there was something unclean about going out and tracking down the principals in a disappearance of this kind.

I knew where Highland was. It was a small rural community about fifteen miles from town. Mary had driven me out through there to the Pryor farm one day to show me a horse. The horse had rolled his eyes, laid his ears back and tried to make a meal off my arm. She had said he was "spirited." I watched from a safe place while John Fidd saddled the horse and Mary took him out and ran him. He was foaming and wilted when she brought him back. Fidd took him and started walking him around. She showed me most of the farm and then we went back to town, with Mary smelling faintly of horse.

The paper had run a cut of Mary. It saddened me to look at it. It had been taken some years ago, before life had put that look of mockery and hardness in her eyes. She looked very young, very earnest.

My girl came in at quarter to nine. Her name is Antonia MacRae. She is a slim pleasant morsel, and satisfyingly bright. She decorates and implements an office adequately. Italian and Scots combine to make an intriguing woman. Her mother gave her her coloring, her suggestively rounded figure with its promise of languor and lazy Sundays in bed. But from Papa she inherited a cool, canny eye, a lot of skepticism, and a brain that goes click like an I.B.M. machine.

She came in wearing a blue jumper over a white blouse. With her crow-wing hair and white white teeth, the effect was good. The beltless waist of the jumper was so beautifully fitted to her figure that, had I not had Mary on my mind, it would have been distracting.

It makes for a peculiar relationship to share an office with a girl who is lovely and desirable, as well as efficient. When work piled up I could forget everything except her quickness and her loyalty. It was during the lulls that I would become aware of other things. As when she would sit on her heels and dig for something in the

bottom drawer of a file cabinet, and I would find myself
staring at the way her waist would curve richly into the
fullness of hips. Or she would bring something to me
at my desk and, out of the corner of my eye, I would
see the impertinence of breast under a sheen of office
blouse, a bare six inches away. Or I would be standing
over her, dictating to her, and, while hunting for the
right phrase, realize I was bobbing my head around
like a fool trying to find a vantage point from where
I could look down the front of her dress.

Toni MacRae was quite aware of my interest, my
speculative admiring interest. It caused her to change
certain postures rather quickly. It often caused a very
delicate blush. I had made a pass the second week she
was in my office. It had been repulsed with unmistakable firmness, and no anger. She made it clear for the
record. Another type of girl in those same circumstances,
quite aware of her figure and of the boss's interest in
it, might have done a certain amount of flaunting and
posturing. Not Toni. She couldn't very well wear a
Mother Hubbard, but she dressed and carried herself so as to minimize office tension.

"Good morning," she said, putting her purse in her
desk drawer.

"Morning. I'm reading about Mary."

"You were one of the friends she had dinner with,
weren't you? I heard you talking to Mr. Raymond about
it Friday."

"I was one of the ones, yes."

"Funny thing," she said, frowning thoughtfully. She
leaned back in her little secretarial chair. Her desk is
cattycorner near the outside windows, facing mine. She
laced her fingers across the nape of her neck, elbows out,
frowning as she thought about Mary's disappearance. I
must have stared at the front of the jumper with horrid
intensity. She straightened up, lowering her arms hastily,
bringing her typing machine up out of the bowels of
the desk with one practiced muscular wrench.

I could sense the plant filling up. I could hear the far-away ding-ding-ding of the I.B.M. time clock as they filed in. A few pieces of equipment started and then, on the stroke of nine the place came to full life for the long Monday. Hangover day. Absentee day. Gus Kruslov was my first customer. He waddled in and said, "I ain't got me a single damn man to put on that number three mill."

"You'll have to take King off setup then."

"He'll raise hell."

"Put him on. Lean on him. I'll stop by later and sweet-talk him."

As soon as he was gone, Ratcher came in with one of his kid engineers who had dreamed up a cutie over the weekend. We spread the drawing out on the table and went over it, and it looked fine. The kid was beaming. Toni had gotten the summary report from the records clerk and she was making a stencil, so I went down on the floor with the engineers.

It was that kind of a day. A jumping bean day. Dodd Raymond came up to my office at about eleven. Toni had spotted him down on the floor and tipped me. He came in and shut the noise out, and glanced at Toni. I told her to go get me that tool list. That was code to go powder her nose.

Dodd placed a haunch on my desk corner, clicked my lamp on and off. "They still don't know a damn thing," he said. "I just talked to Sutton."

"Who would Sutton be?"

"Chief of Police. There isn't enough yet to warrant bringing in the F.B.I. but they're standing by." He glanced at me. "Clint, do you think she could be doing all this for a gag? For excitement. For some kind of a laugh."

"It doesn't seem reasonable to me."

"The police are going to keep digging. Clint, I know it's none of my damn business but were you . . . intimate with her?"

I looked him in the eye. I'd never noticed before how

pale his eyes were. I smiled and said, "I guess that's right."

"What's right?"

"That it's none of your damn business."

He had the grace to flush. He got off my desk and off my back. "Well, maybe we'll know soon."

"Maybe we will."

He left. It annoyed me that he would be sly enough to use the smoke screen of her disappearance to try to find out if she'd been cheating on him. It annoyed me, and yet it planted some serious doubts about the correctness of my bedtime conjectures about him. If he knew she was dead, having killed her, he wouldn't be concerned about her possible promiscuity. Evidently Mary Olan had given him a hell of a time, and I couldn't be precisely sorry.

I had just gotten back from a late lunch, having missed the closing time of the cafeteria by minutes, when Harvey Wills phoned down to me. "Clint, I just had a call from Mr. Willis Pryor. They're having a little conference out at his house this afternoon about this Olan girl. They want you and Dodd there. Dodd has already left. I didn't want either of you to go at first, but Mr. Pryor hinted that it could be made official if I didn't cooperate."

"Hell!"

"Are you loaded up?"

"I'm jammed. Well, I guess I gotta."

I explained the situation to Toni and asked her if she'd mind hanging around after five if I hadn't gotten back by then. She said she wouldn't mind. I told her not to wait beyond six. I had a few instructions and she took them down in her notebook. She looked up at me when I had finished, her eyes serious.

"Clint, does she mean a lot to you?" She calls me Clint when we are alone, never anything but Mr. Sewell when anybody else is there. She flushed and looked away after asking the question.

"Not too much, Toni. She's a spoiled brat. She thinks

she's better than practically anybody else. But . . . it's been something to do in the evening."

"I shouldn't have asked that. But you've been so . . . odd this morning. As if you're very troubled."

"I guess I am." But I couldn't tell her why.

The day was still dismal as I drove out toward the Pryor home. The sky was dark and I wondered if it was raining in the hills. It occurred to me I might have picked the spot too well—it might be a year before anyone found her. Then just the delicate yellowed skull, black hair clinging to dried scrap of scalp. Skirt shredded by the winds and the rain, rotten to the touch. If no one found her, I knew I would live with nightmares for a long, long time.

chapter 5

Though the assemblage was unexpectedly large—eleven already gathered when I walked in—they looked muted and dwarfed by the big dramatic living room. The white fireplace wall was at least twenty feet high. There was just enough edge in the day, with the change of wind, so that a small fire glowed in the waist-high fireplace set into the wall.

Willy Pryor greeted me. He acted nervous, keyed up. He has a heavy shock of white hair which has not receded a bit, though he must be about fifty. His massive white eyebrows curl upward and outward. He is as brown as any Polynesian all year round. His standard costume is riding pants and boots and a cotton shirt unbuttoned halfway to the waist with the sleeves rolled up. The grey hair is thickly matted on his chest. He's about five seven, stocky, trim and powerful, with arms like a stevedore. I guess he has never had to do a day's work in his life, but he does manual labor on the Pryor farm, rides, hunts, flies, goes after marlin and tuna each year. You sense that had it been necessary for him to work, had he started with nothing, he would somehow have ended up just where he is, and just what he is. He's a good talker, a sometimes extravagant personality.

His wife, Myrna, smiled a bit timidly at me. She is a round, warm, dull, comfortable woman. She bore three daughters for Willy, and that seems to have been the extent of her participation in life. No beautician, no couturier could ever make Myrna Pryor look like anything other than precisely what she was—a farm girl from the Highland area. Maybe with his neurotic murderous sister, and all his other highly-charged relatives, Myrna was exactly what Willy had wanted and needed. And it had helped the blood, if the bouncy health of Jigger, Dusty and Skeeter was any indication.

I nodded and spoke to Dodd and Nancy. They sat side by side on a creation neither couch nor chair—something resembling an upholstered coffee table with a back six inches high.

The only other person in the room I knew by sight was the plain clothes partner of the uniformed patrolman who had come to wake me up Sunday morning.

Willy performed the introductions quickly and clearly. The wiry big-handed blonde who looked as if she had been nailed to a barn to dry in the sun was Neale Bettiger, Mary's golf partner. A wide, impassive, sleepy-eyed man was Captain Joseph Kruslov, in charge of the case. I asked him if he was related to Gus at the plant.

"Brother," he said.

A tall, stooped, sick-looking man with grey bags under his eyes was Mr. Stine, Commissioner of Public Safety. The plain clothes cop was named Hilver. Chief of Police Sutton was colorless, rolypoly and asthmatic. When he spoke he honked. Willy skipped over a police stenographer sitting stiffly, uncomfortably at a corner desk and introduced me to a mild little guy sitting off by himself. He looked like a frail bank teller until you took the second look. Then you saw the sardonic cut of the mouth, the alive quick eyes, the unexpected thickness of the wrists. "This is Mr. Paul France. He's a licensed investigator and I've asked him to sit in, with Chief Sutton's permission."

Willy shooed me to a chair next to the sun-dried blonde, rubbed his hands together and said, "Well, Chief, I guess we can get started."

"Captain Kruslov will ask some questions," the chief said.

Kruslov paced to the center of the room. "We called you people together to see if we can come up with anything we missed so far. We're interested mostly in anybody any of you could have seen hanging around, acting funny, anything like that. We're sort of thinking of a snatch. We'll take up this angle first. Miss Bettson?"

"Bettiger. No, I didn't see a thing. Mary and I played twenty-seven holes. At the end of eighteen we were even in holes and even in score so we played another nine. I won three and two. I didn't see a thing out of line."

"How did she act? Same as usual?"

"Oh yes. We gabbed, kidded around, talked about people. She was fine. Nobody was lurking about, if that's what you mean."

"Now will you tell the chief and these people what you told Sergeant Hilver this morning."

Miss Bettiger looked uncomfortable. "Well, I don't think it was important. It was just talk."

"Go ahead, please."

"We talked about men. We do that a lot, I guess, maybe too much. Mary was laughing about what she called her 'reserve love nest.' She said there was this man who had been making a big play and he kept trying to give her a key to a place he had rented somewhere in town. She said if she ever wanted to hide, that would be the place, because he wouldn't dare give her away."

"Did she tell you his name?"

I did not dare look over at Dodd and Nancy. I was afraid of what I'd see on their faces. "No, she didn't tell me his name. She just said he's married. She made a big joke of it."

Kruslov turned to Mr. Pryor. "Mr. Pryor, do you think Miss Olan could be at that apartment or room or house she spoke of to Miss Bettson?"

"Bettiger," the girl said.

"Sorry. Miss Bettiger."

Uncle Willy said hotly, "I think it's a damned outrage to suggest any such thing. Mary is a good girl. She's unpredictable, but basically good. She'd be no part of any cheap arrangement like that. If she was I'd . . . I'd throw her out of my home. I'm raising three daughters here." I saw the bulge of his brown forearms and was convinced.

"I still think we have to consider that as a possibility," Captain Kruslov said. "Now, Mr. and Mrs. Raymond. Did you notice anything at all suspicious about Saturday night?"

They looked at each other and I read Nancy's lips as she said to go ahead. "No," Dodd said. "It was a perfectly standard evening."

"Did Miss Olan drink too much?"

"I . . . well, yes. Frankly, she did."

"Was she in the habit of drinking too much?"

"No."

"Why did she drink so much Saturday?"

"I don't think she intended to. I think she made a mistake ordering. She got thirsty playing golf and she should have started on something tall instead of cocktails."

"Did you witness the quarrel between her and Mr. Sewell?"

"Yes, I did."

"Would you tell us about it?"

"That's very simple. Clint was trying to help her. He wanted her to stop drinking. She got nasty about it, but Clint didn't. He just kept coaxing her and after she made quite a little scene at the bar, she let him lead her out of there. I thought he handled it rather well. It really wasn't anything important."

"A drunken woman is a despicable thing," Willy said firmly. "It is always important."

"I mean the quarrel wasn't important, Mr. Pryor."

"Did you or your wife notice anyone hanging around, or see anything you thought odd at the time?"

"No sir. I guess we left a few minutes before Mr. Sewell left with Miss Olan. I understand he planned to drive her

home and take a cab from here. Later he told me that
. . ."

"Never mind that. You saw nothing out of line."

"No sir."

Kruslov turned to me. He moved closer to me than he had to the others. He looked more intent. I gave him exactly the same story I had given the two cops. He took me over it twice. I didn't especially care for his manner. I wondered if he was getting even for the times I had chewed out his brother.

"So when she drove away you went right to bed."

"I've told you that."

"What time was it?"

"Two-thirty. Something like that."

"You went right to sleep."

"Yes. I was tired."

"Your landlady says you didn't get in until four."

"Does she? I can't help that. I was in by two-thirty, and asleep by no later than two-thirty-five. She must be mistaken."

"She is positive that a car drove in at four."

"Captain, I'm a very sound sleeper. Your sergeant over there can verify that. It is entirely possible that one of my less responsible friends drove in at four and couldn't wake me and drove away again."

He dropped that line and went back to the questions he had asked the others. "Did you see anything suspicious? Did any car follow you? Anything like that?"

"No, I didn't see . . ."

"What's the matter?"

"I just remembered something. Mary and I sat out in her car in my driveway for a few minutes and talked. Somebody came into the driveway, backed out and went away. I figured they were just turning around. I just now remembered it."

Kruslov gave a grunt of satisfaction. "There's a new fact. It could mean something. Did the car lights shine on you?"

"Yes they did. The top was down. I'll tell you more than I have to, Captain. At the moment we were illuminated, I happened to be kissing Miss Olan."

"Are you in love with her?"

"I wouldn't say that. I kiss her goodnight. Now here's some more while we're at it. We made a date to go up to the lake yesterday. I went anyway, thinking she'd show up. She was going to pick me up at noon. It was entirely possible that I would have been pounding my ear, so I gave her a key. I went in and got it, and took it out to her. So that if I was still sleeping she could come in and drag me out of the sack so we wouldn't be held up. But I assure you, Captain, that the key I gave her is not the love nest key she spoke to Miss Bettiger about. I had no such designs on Miss Olan. No, that doesn't sound right. I had designs, I'm that normal. But they didn't include setting up a menage of that special type."

The phone on the free form desk rang. The police stenographer jumped, picked it up timidly, spoke into it in an inaudible voice.

He held the phone out. "For you, Captain sir."

Kruslov walked heavily over and took the phone. "Yes . . . ? Yes . . . I see . . . Where . . . ? No, that's okay . . . Yes, I'll tell them."

He hung up. He had his own little sense of drama. He walked back to the middle of the room and said, "They found her."

"Is she all right?" Uncle Willy asked.

"She was strangled to death. Probably some time Saturday night. Her body was dumped in the brush up in the hills, a half mile or so off the main road. Damnedest thing. There was a troop of Brownies on a hike yesterday. What the hell are Brownies? One little girl wandered off and saw the body and was too scared to tell anybody. Today she was so upset her mother finally got her to talk and drove her up there to prove it was just the little girl's imagination. But it wasn't. She got hold of the state troopers."

In the long silence Willy said softly, "Oh my God."

Myrna leaned forward and put her face in her hands. Her shoulders shook gently. I looked over at the Raymonds. Nancy held her head high, her face tilted slightly upward. From a long high window, a sort of skylight effect, the light of the pale grey day came down, touching the delicacy of her face, the parted lips. Cherry glow of fire made a highlight on the soft line of her jaw. It was a face almost without expression, clear, clean and perfect. If there was any expression, it was as though she listened for some expected sound. Dodd sat with his head bent, staring at his large clenched fist as though he held something small there, captive.

Stine had a high weak voice. "Willy, I'll tell you this. I'll tell you this definitely. And Jud Sutton will back me up, I know. No man assigned to this case is going to get a complete night's rest until we've got the person or persons who did this thing."

"I appreciate that, Tom," Willy Pryor said in a low voice. He turned and faced the fire, hard brown hands locked behind him.

Kruslov broke into the mood with his heavy factual voice. "We'll forget the kidnaping angle for right now. Let's all put our heads together as long as we're here and figure out who might want to kill that girl. Who hates her?"

Miss Bettiger, surprisingly, was the one who answered. "I guess I, or nearly anybody who knew Mary, could make out a list of the people who didn't like her. She didn't go around trying to make friends. She had a lot of friends, but she snubbed a lot of people. Phonies, mostly. People who wanted to be seen with her and sponge off her. She got that income from the trust funds and . . ."

"How much income?" Kruslov asked.

Willy, without turning, said, "Sixty thousand a year. She didn't throw it away. She had her own investment program. Got money sense from her father, I guess. She was getting a good return from her own investments and reinvesting that too."

"Who gets it now?" Kruslov asked. I could understand why Stine and Sutton had brought him along. He could ask the ugly questions they couldn't ask because of their personal relationship with the Pryors.

Willy turned and gave him a look of mild surprise. "I guess that what the government doesn't get will stay in the family. We'll get it. If I remember Rolph's will correctly, it set up trust funds for Nadine, John and Mary. I guess Rolph considered each settlement ample, because in the case of the death of any of them—the children without issue—Myrna and I, or our children, were named as residual legatees."

"Wouldn't he have wanted to leave it all to his kids, to the survivor?" Kruslov asked.

Willy's face hardened. "I have no idea what was in his mind, my good man. It may be that he remembered, at the time he made out his will, that he married Pryor money at a time when he needed it very badly to save the Olan interests. Perhaps he felt that it was proper, after providing for his wife and children adequately, to see that in case of common disaster or the death of any of them, the money would revert to the Pryor family. The Citizens Bank and Trust acts as executor. If you check with them you will find that the estate has not been entirely settled, even after sixteen years, due to the unfortunate illness of my sister. Furthermore, Captain, I can assure you that we do not need the money. I assume you can check that fact somehow."

Kruslov refused to be backed down. I had to admire his stolid dignity. "Thanks for the information, Mr. Pryor. I will have to have a list of the men Miss Olan has been going out with."

"I can tell you that," Miss Bettiger said. "At least I can tell you who she's gone out with since she got back from Spain in February."

"How long was she in Spain?"

"Six months," Willy said. "I disapproved of her going on a trip like that alone. She was restless. I couldn't stop her."

Bettiger frowned into the fire. "Let's see. Bill Mulligan. Don Rhoades. Mr. Sewell." She looked apprehensively at Willy. "There's one other, but . . ."

"But what?" Kruslov asked, moving closer to her.

"I don't want to get him in trouble."

"I'll have to know that name, Miss Bettson."

She looked at Kruslov with exasperation, but didn't correct him. "All right, but there goes a good job. Nels Yeagger."

Willy's brown face turned the color of a brick. "That's a damn lie!"

"It's not a damn lie!" Miss Bettiger shrilled. "And don't try to call me a liar, Willy Pryor."

"Who is this guy?" Kruslov demanded.

"He works at our place at Smith Lake," Willy said. "He takes care of the boats and does odd jobs. Mary wouldn't . . ."

"But she did," Bettiger said. "She went out with him quite a few times. She'd drive up there and meet him before you opened the place at the lake. He was crazy about her. She told me about it. She stopped going out with him because she said he had started to bore her. He was beginning to act jealous and possessive, and that was the one thing Mary never could stand."

Kruslov said, as though speaking to himself, "The body wasn't far off the main road between here and Smith Lake. Jealous." He turned and nodded at Hilver. Hilver left his post by the far wall and headed toward the door.

At the door Hilver stopped and said, "The state boys?"

"No. This is ours. Take Watson along and pick him up yourself and bring him in. Any more, Miss Bettiger?"

"No more that I know of. I think I know them all. We . . . always told each other everything. Gosh, it's going to seem kind of . . ." She dived into her purse for a handkerchief.

The more I thought about it, the better Yeagger fitted the role of murderer. He'd seen me with her up there at the lake. And I remembered a rather awkward little incident. It had happened the first time I went there with her. We were looking for somebody, I forget who. We'd walked up to the horse barn. Mary was wearing slacks. When she went in ahead of me I told her that she'd missed one of her belt loops in the back. She had stopped at once and said, "So fix it!"

She undid her belt and I pulled it back through the loops and threaded it through the one she had missed. Then I had reached my arms around her and I had just started fumbling with the belt buckle when Yeagger walked into the barn. He'd stopped quickly. Mary had said hello to him, moved out of my arms and buckled her own belt. Even at the time I realized that it must have looked damn funny to Yeagger, because he had no way of knowing how we had gotten into that situation—my arms around her, a pile of straw handy, and her belt undone. I realized now that it must have driven him crazy, finding us like that. Apparently she had stopped seeing him, and he was jealous.

It wasn't too hard to imagine him driving down into the city on Saturday night and hunting for her. He could very easily have spotted her car at the club. He looked like a man with a lot of patience. He could have followed us. It could have been Nels Yeagger who put the car lights on us. He was born and raised in the woods; it would have been no trouble for him to park up the street and come back silently through the grass. Maybe just in time to hear me give her the key. The rest would not have been hard to arrange, and he had provocation.

It made me feel better about my part of it. I hadn't done anything. The body had been found. If Yeagger had done it, and I was growing more convinced every moment that he had, they would break him down and my part would be forgiven in the triumph of catching him.

After a few more questions which uncovered nothing,

the meeting broke up. Myrna Pryor had already left the room, right after Kruslov gave the account of the phone call. I walked out into the grey afternoon with Nancy and Dodd.

"She was so very much alive," Dodd murmured.

"And now she is so very much dead," Nancy said too sharply. I looked at her. I did not like the look in her eyes. She was not a nice woman at that moment.

They drove off. As I stopped on the way toward my car to light a cigarette, Paul France caught up with me. He wore a pale grey felt hat with the brim turned up all the way around. It was pushed back a little. He looked like a mild rabbit.

"You like Yeagger for it," he said.

"What do you mean?"

"Her kid brother hired me, Sewell. I sat and watched people. Don't ever play poker with me. You came into that room and you held a straight open in the middle with all your money on the table. Then the call came. For you it was like a one card draw that filled that belly straight. You lost the lines in your face and your shoulders dropped a good two inches with relief."

"You have quite an imagination."

"I have none. I never believe anything I don't see. That's maybe why I do good at this business."

"Maybe I was afraid Kruslov was aiming at me, Mr. France."

"Was that all?"

"I don't see how it could be anything else, do you?"

He smiled at me. I did not like his smile. There are certain sharp-toothed tropical fish that wear that same smile all the time. He went back toward the house. He wore a rumpled blue suit that looked too big for him. I watched the way he moved. Bullfighters move that way, and very good dancers, and top ring professionals. I was glad he had broken off the conversation, he made me uncomfortable. I was particularly glad I hadn't killed her. France had a certain gothic menace about him. And his eyes were as wise and ancient and knowing as those of a great lizard.

It was ten of six when I turned into the plant road. Just as I made the turn the black sky opened and the rain sluiced down, lifting a six-inch fringe of silver off the asphalt, so heavy that the wipers were useless. As I crept cautiously along I saw Toni MacRae, distorted by the windshield water, galloping along the side of the road toward the bus stop, holding her purse over her head. The rain had caught her midway between the plant and the bus stop shelter.

She ran girl-fashion, knees in, heels kicking out, hips switching. It is awkward, and sometimes ludicrous, often charming. There seems an unpleasant distortion about any girl who runs as a boy runs.

I swung the car door open and yelled at her. She ran for the car, grabbed the door handle, swung herself in and plumped down on the seat, slamming the car door in the same motion. She was panting and she smelled of damp cloth and damp girl.

"Glub," she said.

"Bad timing."

"Another fifty feet and I could have stopped running. It wouldn't have made any difference then. I thought I could make it to the shelter before it hit. Bad guess. Gosh, I'm soaking."

The jumper was a darker blue and a closer fit. The white blouse showed pink where rain had pasted it to her arms. Her hair was fairly dry right on top, but the ends were drenched. At the plant I swung around and headed back out toward the road.

"This time I get to take you home," I said.

"This time," she agreed. It was a standing argument between us, her not letting me drive her to or from work. She lives in a rooming house at 985 Jefferson. My apartment is at 989, just two doors away. I hadn't known she was in the neighborhood until I had seen her one Sunday afternoon at the corner store. Then she told me the story. Her father lives with his second wife on the other side of town. He stayed single for several years after Toni's mother died, and then married again. The house is small and there was a new crop of children. Toni moved out, with no ill will on either side. It was a question of space, primarily.

"Is there anything new about Mary Olan?" she asked.

"They found her body. She was strangled. They found the body north of here, in the woods."

"How awful!" Toni said. "How perfectly dreadful! Who did it?"

"They don't know. They think a handyman named Yeagger did it." I told her why they thought he might have done it.

She sneezed three times, making of each small paroxysm a delectable thing indeed. I turned on the car heater. She pulled off her sodden shoes and curled nyloned toes in the direct heat.

"Poor Mary Olan," she said.

"I don't know, Toni. I really don't know. She had health and money and position. But she didn't seem to be having a very good time. She wasn't enjoying herself. She had a set of demons riding her, making with the spurs and flailing the whips."

The rain slackened a bit but as I turned into our street it came down again harder than before, making floods in the gutters and a metallic hammering on the car roof over our heads, turning the car into a small isolated world. I parked in her driveway, and when she reached for the door handle I said, "Relax a minute. It'll ease up. No need to get a worse soaking. I've got no place to go."

We sat there in the rain. Slow traffic crept by, headlights shining. I said, "I'll start this old phonograph record again. Why can't I drive you to work and back. You'd save money and you'd get fifteen extra minutes sleep in the morning."

She smiled at me. "You could almost sell me on that sleep thing. But no, Clint. Thanks, but no."

It irritated me a little, because of the inference that I made the offer with ulterior motives. "Why not?" I asked, too harshly over the tin drumming of the rain.

"Strange things happen to the local C.P.P. girls who date the fair-haired boys who get shipped in here, Clint. They seem to get fired, and I like my work. Any more questions?" She had matched my harshness with her anger.

"Just a ride to and from work. What's wrong with that?"

She looked at me speculatively, lips pursed. "Just a ride. That's it, isn't it? For now. Be practical, Clint, please. We're both lonely. I'm aware of that and I guess you are. Just a ride, to work every morning and home every night. And every night I get out neatly and say thanks. Is that what you think? How soon before we'd stop on the way home? Just a cup of coffee, Tina. Sure. Later a steak. Fine. No, Clint. We keep this formal. We work in the same office. That's all and that's all there will be, because I like you too much already."

She had worked her feet into her damp shoes while she spoke. She opened the car door and was gone, running through the rain, up onto the front porch of the old yellow house. She gave a shy wave and went inside.

I forgot everything else she said and remembered only that she had said she liked me too much already. It was the first chink in cool armor. I suspected that she had said it impulsively and would be sorry later. Tina was not one to plot, to connive a chance to say a thing like that.

I went home and thought about her, about long quick legs and the tilt of her smile, about eyes that held gravity and shyness.

chapter 6

My local sonorous evening commentator said in part, at ten o'clock that evening, "Chief of Police Judson Sutton told your reporter earlier this evening that he expects an early solution to the brutal murder of Mary Olan. Rain and darkness prevented as thorough a search of the area where the body was found as was desired. The roped off and guarded area will be searched again in the morning in the hope that some clue can be found that will point to the identity of the murderer."

I hoped they would not look in any holes in rotten birch trees.

"Earlier today Nels Yeagger, handyman at the Pryor estate at Smith Lake was brought down to the city for questioning. He was picked up by two of the men assigned to Captain Kruslov, who is handling the case personally. At the time of this broadcast Yeagger has not yet been released, and it is assumed that he is still being interrogated.

"The coroner's office, after an examination of the body, has established the time of death as some time between two A.M. and five A.M. Sunday morning. Death was caused by a thin band of fabric that was tightened around the throat. There is no indication that the fabric was knotted. Coroner Walther stated that the object used could have been a belt used as a slip noose. The actual throat injury was slight, and it is believed that strangulation took place slowly. The absence of any marks of conflict on the body seem to indicate that the girl was unconscious at the time she was killed. She had not been criminally attacked. The body was taken to the place where it was found in a car, and the tire marks were carefully obliterated where the car passed over soft bare ground. An extremely valuable wristwatch had not been removed from the body, and police have eliminated robbery as a motive, despite the fact that the dead girl's purse has not yet been found. At the dinner party before her death she was carrying a small black envelope purse with a gold clasp. She . . ."

My phone rang and I turned the radio down. It was Hilver. "Mr. Sewell, the captain wants you should come down and leave off fingerprints. I was supposed to tell you today out at Pryor's but he sent me off and I forgot about it."

"Right now?"

"Right now."

There isn't any answer to that. I agreed, put my tie and jacket back on and went on down to police headquarters. It is a grimy old red stone building, full of the varied stinks of a hundred years of crime and punishment. A sergeant behind a wicket told me where to go. A bored man wrote down my name, age, height, weight, marital status, employment, and place of birth. He rolled my fingers on an ink pad and then on a printed card. When he was through he gave me one paper towel and sent me over to a chipped sink in the corner of the room.

"Can I go now?"

"Sit down over there," he said. I sat. He left the room. I sat and sat. There was an electric clock on the wall. Every two minutes it clacked loudly, jumped forward two minutes and caught up with Time. A garage girl on a wall calendar had snared her skimpy skirt crawling through a barbed wire fence. Some jokester had given her a complete set of hirsute adornment. I kept yawning so hard I shuddered. I got sick of looking at the wooden floor, one high table, one low table, four chairs, the tan institutional plaster wall. Sometimes people would walk down the hall, by the open door. That, at least, was mildly entertaining. A sniffling girl went by once, a short fat matron prodding her in the back with a bitter knuckle. Another time a man started whooping and yelling and roaring. He stopped in the middle of a roar, stopped very, very abruptly. A young cop went by trying to sing.

At eleven-thirty Kruslov came in. He was in shirt-sleeves, his tie untied, the two ends hanging down in discouraged fashion. He stared at me, obviously puzzled. He turned on his heel and left. I called after him but he didn't answer.

Ten minutes later he came back with a sheet of paper in his hand, studying it. He sat on the low table. "Sewell. Let's see what we got. Clear print of first and second finger of left hand on rear of side mirror, smudged print of left thumb on face of mirror. Section of print of right thumb, clear, on horn ring." He put the paper aside and stared at me.

"I told you I drove the car," I said angrily. "I adjusted the side mirror. I guess I blew the horn once. Now you've proved I've driven the car."

He yawned and stuck a fist against his mouth. "Relax. Relax. You shouldn't have been told to stay around."

"Can I go now?"

"Gus says you're a working fool. He says you spend more time on his back than off it."

"Gus and I get along."

"He said that too. He hasn't missed a day, except vacations, since they opened that plant. Twenty years around machines, the last six at that place."

"He's a good man."

He yawned again. "I should have gone into that racket. I figured this would give me retirement. Now Gus gets retirement too, maybe better than I do. What's there left to make a man go on the cops?"

"Has Yeagger confessed?"

"No. We're letting him go. It took a long time to

check, but it checked out finally. We had to contact half
the people in the hills. He quit work Saturday at six.
He spent from eight to midnight in a beer joint. Then
he and another guy picked up two girls who came into
the beer joint. They had a car and a bottle. They went
to a hunting camp up near Grey Lake and stayed right
there until noon Sunday. This Yeagger had tied on such
a load he was pretty shaggy about the details. But we
got it all checked out. He wouldn't say anything for a
while, until we convinced him he was in bad trouble.
He didn't want to talk because there is going to be some
trouble with the husband of one of the two girls they
picked up. You know something funny? He says this
and I believe him. It's the first time in his whole life he
ever did anything like that. How about that?"

"Rough."

"He loses his job because the Olan girl went out with
him. He gets in a big jam. It's a real mess for that boy. He
got drunk on account of the Olan girl."

"Is that what he says?"

"I believe that, too. You know, that little girl was a bad
actor. The more I dig, the more I find out. She went up
there before her uncle opened the place at the lake just to
make trouble for Yeagger. She took him back to the
place. She had a key. She took him in there and taught
him most of the facts of life in one big lesson. Getting
that out of him was like pulling teeth. She went up a
few more times, got him all mixed up and involved, and
then dropped him like he was dirt."

"I'll be damned."

"You know, he hates you, Sewell. He thinks you took
her away from him. He thinks you were getting what
he was missing."

"I wasn't. But it wasn't for lack of trying, Captain."

"I can believe that. I saw her alive a couple times. Nice
little piece. Even dead she doesn't look too bad. Here's a
funny thing. This Yeagger thought Willy Pryor knew
what was going on."

"I can hardly believe that."

"I don't believe it. He says he got that impression from something the Olan girl said to him. He can't remember just what it was. He thinks she said Willy Pryor knew everything she did. That she told him, or something like that. As if she bragged to him."

"She must have been just talking."

"I figure it that way. Sewell, you didn't drop that body off on your way to the lake, did you?"

My heart took a fast uppercut at the back of my throat and dropped back lower than where it belonged. Then I saw that he was half smiling.

"I didn't want to get my car messed up. I dragged the body along behind."

"I sure wish I knew who lugged her up there. It wasn't Yeagger. You go on home and get your sleep, Sewell."

He walked out with me. We stood near the door chatting when Yeagger came through, being escorted toward the door by Hilver. They had apparently grabbed him in his work clothes and he was still in them. He was overwhelmingly big, well over six feet tall, and physically hard. Thigh muscles bulged the tight jeans. He looked surly, weary, discouraged.

He recognized me and his face changed. He looked away quickly and went on out the front door. Hilver stood and watched him go. The door swung shut.

"How'll he get back?" Kruslov asked.

"I asked him. He says he'll get back. I guess he's big enough to take care of himself."

The three of us chatted for a few moments and then I left. It was well after midnight and the town was asleep. It is pretty much of a Saturday night town. I walked to my car. I knew that Yeagger was out here in the night. I remembered the way he had looked at me, and it made the back of my neck feel odd. I walked slower than I wanted to, to prove to myself that I wasn't frightened.

My car was parked too far from the nearest street light. As I took my keys out of my pocket, a big shadow de-

tached itself from the darker mass of my car and stood
blocking the way.

"Yeagger?" I said. The night street was too empty, and
my voice was too thin.

He called me a foul name and leaped toward me. I
struck at him and hit an arm like an oak limb. He caught
my wrist and twisted it. It spun me around, my wrist
and hand pinned high between my shoulder blades. I've
never felt frail or inadequate, but he handled me as easily
as I'd handle a child. There was a thick sour smell of
sweat about him. The pain in my arm made me gasp.

"Key to the car," he said. I dropped my keys on the
sidewalk. I thought he would let go of me to pick them
up. I intended to run; he looked too muscle-bound to be
able to run as fast as I intended to. But he bent me over
with him as he picked up the keys. He opened the car
door and shoved me in, past the steering wheel, and
climbed in after me.

"Don't try to get out," he said.

"What do you want?"

"I want to talk to you, Sewell. But not here."

"How about my place?" I suggested.

He thought that over. "Who's there?"

"There's nobody there."

He found the right key and drove my car. I gave him
the directions. I didn't know what I should do—he had
started with painful violence, but he sounded reasonable.
Maybe he just wanted to talk. I sensed that I could get
the door open and get out of the car before he could
grab me. We turned into my drive. He turned off the
lights and motor and caught my wrist again. He forced
me out my side of the car, following me. He looked toward
the apartment door. I had left the lights on. He marched
me over into the darkness of the side lot, twisted my wrist
up into my back and cursed me again.

"What do you want?" I asked, fighting to keep my
voice level and unafraid.

He didn't want to talk with me, he wanted to tell me.

He told me I had taken her away from him. He told me she was dead and it was my fault. He kept his voice low, his mouth close to my ear. I sensed that he was losing control. He told me I had to keep away from her. I felt lost and helpless. In his increasing excitement he was close to breaking my arm. I groaned with pain, wishing I had tried to get away from him while we were in the car. I knew my arm would snap. I tried to yell for help, hoping to arouse somebody, hoping to frighten him, or startle him back to relative sanity. He caught my throat, choking off the yell, his heavy forearm across my throat, big knee digging into the small of my back. I managed to turn in his grasp and we both fell. He grasped my throat in his big hands. My right arm was useless. Red pinwheels circled behind my eyes and somebody turned the night off, the way you turn off a light.

When I recovered consciousness I was flat on my back in the night, on the grass, looking up at stars through the May leaves of the elms, my throat hurting with each breath. I could hear heavy breathing close by. After a long time I sat up. Yeagger was beside me on his face, blood on his cheek shining black in the faint starlight.

I massaged my right arm; it felt weak and limp. I wobbled a bit when I stood up. I felt as though someone watched me from the deep shadows under the trees. I managed to roll Yeagger over onto his back. He grunted and threw a big forearm across his eyes. After a long time he sat up and stared at me blankly. I helped him to his feet. He leaned on me heavily and I took him into the apartment. He sat in a chair, elbows on his knees, eyes closed. I moved the light so I could see his head. Above his left temple there was a split in the scalp about an inch long. The area around it was badly swollen. I wet the end of a towel in the bathroom sink and brought it to him. He wiped the blood from his face and held the towel against the slowly bleeding wound.

"What happened?" I asked. I had to ask him twice before he looked directly at me.

"I . . . I guess I was trying to kill you. I heard somebody behind me. I started to turn and . . . that's all."

"It's a damn good thing somebody stopped you," I said.

He looked at me and frowned. "I . . . Everything is shot. Everything. Mary was the one thing that meant anything. You were the one who . . ."

"I didn't do a damn thing. She was a tramp, Yeagger. You were just temporary fun and games. If it meant a hell of a lot to you, that just made the game more interesting. Blame yourself, don't blame me."

He looked away from me. "I guess I know that. I guess I knew it all along. But . . . I'm sorry I went after you and . . ." Astonishingly, the big tough face crumpled, twisted up like a child's, and he began to cry. It made me acutely embarrassed. He covered his eyes with a big hand and sobbed harshly. After a time he stopped, and knuckled his eyes. He wouldn't look toward me again. I told him he ought to have a stitch taken in his head; he said it didn't matter. I asked him how he'd get back up to the lake country; he said that didn't matter either. He was anxious to go. If he hadn't been hit he would have killed me. But I could no longer feel indignation or anger. I felt sorry for him. Big and hard as he was, he was a child underneath. He blamed me for breaking his toys, that was all. I stood out in the drive and watched him walk to the street and turn toward town, a big shadow fading into the night.

I looked out toward the lot and felt again that someone was there. It was an atavistic quiver of warning, legacy from the days of the sabertooth. The world was suddenly dark and large and unfriendly. Yeagger had been eliminated. Someone, for an unknown reason, had halted a murder. On this night I could believe it had been halted only to be consummated later, by someone else. I went in to bed and wondered if it would have mattered to anyone if my life had ended there with Yeagger's hands on my throat. It could so easily have ended—and my last conscious perception would have been of the rockets behind my eyes and the world turned off by a monster switch.

The feeling of depression was still with me the next morning when I awoke. My arm was lame, but more serviceable than I had expected. My throat was sore, my voice husky. The episode with Yeagger seemed like a dream sequence, too unreal to reawaken fear. During all my dreams that night, someone had stood in shadow and watched me.

As I went out my driveway I saw Mrs. Speers standing in a window. I remembered that I had not collected her trash.

At the plant the floor was ready for two new pieces of heavy equipment. Two experts were there from the machine tool company. It took half the morning to set the equipment in place, make the power hookups and bolt it down. Then we went over it with Gus and with engineering and the experts until we knew all the tricks. At three I still hadn't had lunch. I went to the locker room, took the protective coveralls off, scoured the grease off my hands and put my suit coat on.

Dodd Raymond came in. He seemed vague, distracted. "Understand they let Yeagger go," he said.

"That's right. Last night. I was there."

"What were you doing down there, Clint?"

"They wanted fingerprints. Did they get yours?"

"Yes. That Paul France stopped in at the house last night. Asked a lot of questions. Strange sort of guy."

I finished drying my hands and turned to face him. "Did he ask about the key the Bettiger woman mentioned?"

"Why should he?"

"Dodd, Mary told me about you and the key and your little hideaway."

He flushed angrily. "She promised not to say anything to anybody."

"You were pretty foolish, weren't you?"

I saw his face change. "Don't forget yourself, Sewell."

"Forget you're the boss? No. But what do I say if I'm asked about it?"

He immediately became ingratiating. "Clint, I didn't mean to get stuffy. Actually, it wouldn't help the police any to tell them that. If she told you, you know I had a place on the west side of town. I'm going to get my stuff out of there as soon as I get a chance. It was a damn fool thing to do. But I lost my head, I guess. We met there six or seven times, that's all. It wouldn't help the police, and it might break up my home. Nancy doesn't know anything about it. I'd appreciate it if you'd just . . . let it ride. After all, I didn't kill her. That ought to be pretty obvious."

"So who did kill her, Dodd?"

He moved over to a mirror, straightened his necktie. "I haven't any idea," he said. But I saw his eyes in the mirror. I sensed that he lied. Maybe he didn't actually know, but I think he had an idea. A good idea.

After he extracted my half-hearted promise not to mention it, he left. I went back to my office. Toni and I had been slightly awkward with each other all day, and I had covered up by being intensely impersonal. Now hunger gnawed at my nerves and I snarled at her, and saw her eyes fill with tears as she turned hastily away. I apologized to her, tried to get her to smile. It was a cool little smile at first, and then it turned into the grin that was so good to see. She went out and brought me back milk and a sandwich.

Nancy Raymond phoned me at five o'clock. She wanted to talk to me but wouldn't say what it was about. She wanted me to meet her at Raphael's, a little place on Broad, not far from the bridge. I agreed.

Toni finished up at about twenty after five. I walked out onto the catwalk and looked down at the big silent production area. I watched Toni walk down the walk toward the iron staircase. She wore a brown linen suit with a burnt orange scarf knotted around her neck. Her long legs swung nicely, hips moving firmly under brown linen, dark head held high. She went out of sight down the circular stairs, heels tamping the metal—and reappeared below. She smiled up at me, flash of white teeth in shadowed face, and then she was gone. I heard the muted distant bell as she punched out.

Raphael's is a logical outgrowth of the new money that has come to town. It is a small place, wedged in where there was logically no room for it. It is ten feet wide and quite deep. Forty feet from the front door it makes a right angle turn and widens out to twenty feet. A zebra-striped spinet piano sits in the angle, dividing the bar from the lounge. During the cocktail hour a girl with lovely bare shoulders sits at the piano, facing a tilted mirror that is placed in the angle of the wall in such a way that from bar or lounge you can see her face and her clever fingers. The lighting is muted, the soundproofing dense, the chairs deep. People talk softly there, drink quietly, and make little schemes that break hearts.

Nancy smiled at me from a corner of the lounge as I walked toward her. She looked as though she had been there some time. She had done something severe with her hair and it made her head look too small.

The waiter came over to the table as I sat. All the other tables were occupied. I asked for a martini. He replaced the ashtray, took Nancy's empty glass and eased away.

"I've had two for courage, Clint," she said. "No, don't look like that. I'm not going to make problems for you like I did that time at the club."

"I wouldn't mind if you did. Old reliable Clint."

"Yes you would mind. And so would I. I don't know . . . how to start this."

"Just start."

She paused while the drinks came. "I told you that we quarreled and Dodd went out and didn't come back until five. Remember that?"

"Yes, of course."

"I guess you're the only person who knows that. He picked me up yesterday to take me out to Pryor's and on the way out he said, very reasonably, that if something had happened to Mary, it might cause a lot of unnecessary talk and trouble if he had to account for that period of time. He told me that he had driven out of town, maybe fifty or sixty miles. He said he had parked beside the road and smoked and listened to the car radio. He said that he was merely sulking like a child, and wanted me to be worried about him. He hadn't seen anyone. He said that after he was there about an hour, he turned around and came home, a little ashamed of himself. He said it would be a lot simpler if I would say that we had gone right home from the club and he hadn't gone out at all."

"You agreed to that?"

"Wait a minute. I said I would think about it. I said that I didn't think it was wise to tell lies to the police. I said if I lied and they found out I had lied, it might make him look worse. Well, you know what happened at that meeting. It certainly seemed to me that Nels Yeagger had done it and they'd prove it—I just had that feeling. So when Sergeant Hilver asked me, I told him just what Dodd wanted me to say. Last night that Paul France came by the house. I told the same lie again. You saw the morning paper. They released Nels."

"Yes?"

She lifted her glass in an uncertain hand. "Clint, I just don't know what to think any more."

"Are you trying to say this? Are you trying to say that now you're wondering if he could have killed her? And you want me to tell you that's nonsense?"

She looked down and when she looked up again, I heard tears in her voice. One tear rolled down her cheek and she wiped at it quickly with the back of her hand, a child's appealing gesture. "I just don't know any more.

I just don't know. And I don't know anyone else to talk to."

"What has started you wondering?"

"He's been . . . so very strange. He hasn't been himself, I guess not since we came here to Warren. Last night he was up most of the night, pacing around. He doesn't hear me when I speak to him."

I told her of my conversation with him in the washroom. Perhaps I should have edited it.

"Six or seven times," she said, a bitter expression on her mouth. "And I know nothing about it. Nothing at all. I suppose these things should have a mathematical value. Six or seven is better than twenty. But one is equal to a hundred, isn't it?"

"I can't see him killing her, Nancy. Not Dodd. He'd risk an affair, but not a murder. He's too cold to risk murder. Too cold and too hard and too ambitious and . . . perhaps too selfish."

I had hoped to comfort her. It was the wrong way. Her eyes flashed. "How can you say that? How can you say a thing like that? People have always liked him and always liked working with him. You're entirely wrong about him. Entirely!"

I thought of Tory's warning, and Ray's warning. I could have told her, but I realized that she didn't have much left. By telling her I would be taking away one more thing, the illusion he had created in her mind. Even though he had hurt her dreadfully with infidelity, she perhaps had a right to be proud of his professional makeup.

"Maybe I'm wrong about that, Nancy."

"You are, Clint."

It surprised me a little that Nancy had never been aware of his ruthlessness in business. He had pretended with her, as with everyone else. I wondered if there was anyone he showed his real face to. I wondered if he had been frank with Mary Olan.

She shivered. "It's awful of me to keep wondering if he

could have done it. If he acted normal, I wouldn't keep
wondering. But he has something on his mind—something so important he seems far away, as if I don't really
know him any more."

"It may be that he's just afraid of the police finding out
about the affair."

"I've thought of that," she said eagerly. "Clint, he
couldn't kill anybody, could he?"

"I don't think so."

She was happier for a moment, and then relapsed again
into worry. She laughed, and it was an unhappy sound.
"Six months ago," she said, "I would have sworn that it
was impossible that he'd ever . . . look for someone
else. But he did. So what good is confidence?"

"There's one way you can end the tension, Nancy."

"How?"

"Tell Kruslov the truth about the night Mary was
killed. He'll find out if Dodd killed her."

She looked at me blankly for what seemed a long time.
She put on her gloves. "Thanks for listening to me, Clint.
I thought you'd be able to help me. I'm sorry I was
wrong."

I watched her leave and sat down again. Poor Nancy.
Her vast capacity for loyalty was at war with the hurt he
had dealt her. She was a woman who seemed to have a
face and a mind planned for a narrower, frailer body.
There was something almost cumbersome about the rich-
ness of her body, as though it burdened her, troubled her,
astonished her. As though it waited patiently, in thrall to
the more pallid mind, yet knowing that when its inevitable moments came, it would once again, as so many
times in the past, take full strong command of the total
organism.

It was easy to sense that with her, physical love was a
complete fulfillment, honestly given, honestly accepted.
Betrayal struck her more deeply that it would a wife who
merely endured the assault of the flesh. The completion
she had found with him had given her a loyalty of mind

and body as well. A loyalty too strong to admit any genuine suspicion that he could have done murder. She teased herself with speculation, punished herself with suspicion that was never deep nor honest.

I signaled for another drink. I watched the bare velvet of the shoulders of the piano girl. She had a style like Previn. I drank up, paid the check and left.

chapter 7

That was Tuesday evening. I fed my martini hunger on spaghetti al dente with sailor sauce, read the evening paper's rehash of our big murder and went back to my apartment. I parked the car, started toward my door, then decided to walk off the spaghetti heaviness. It was just getting dark. Children shrilled and leaped the barberry hedges. I walked by the yellow house and wondered which window was Toni's.

I guess I walked aimlessly for nearly an hour, turning right or left on impulse, but gradually circling back toward my place. I suddenly remembered the trash, and my promise to Mrs. Speers. It wouldn't be too late. I lengthened my stride. From far up the street I saw the lights in my windows. I hadn't been in to leave any on. I left the sidewalk and started across the grass of the big side lawn. I planned to stare in my windows and see who it was who felt so much at home. One key was in my pocket. I had given the other to Mary Olan, and it had been used to put her in my closet. It made me feel strange to see the lights.

When I moved further to the side I saw something that stopped me. It was a silhouette between me and my lighted window. The hat shape was official and distinctive and unmistakable. A police car was parked beside my car, and a policeman stood quietly in the night, leaning against my car.

I moved to put the safe wide trunk of a big elm between me and the waiting man. It took me closer to him. When bright headlights swung into the driveway, I moved again to keep the elm between me and the lights. It was a noisy vehicle and when it turned, I saw that it was a tow truck. I could see men moving around inside my apartment. The door opened and Captain Kruslov stood in the doorway and looked out. He walked out into the driveway and a thin man followed him.

The tow truck backed into position by my car and when its motor quieted I heard Kruslov saying, " . . . and Bird can finish the apartment. You ride on in with the car, Danny, and get to work on the trunk right away. See if you can find anything else."

That "else" chilled my blood. The chain from the hoist on the wrecker clinked against the front bumper of my car. A man got the hook in place, the hoist whined and the front end lifted off the ground. The thin man got into the truck beside the driver and it went away, my car swaying behind it.

Kruslov watched it go. The patrolman who had been leaning against my car stood beside him. Light shone from my open front door. Into the light came Mrs. Speers, a shawl around her shoulders.

"Did you take Mr. Sewell's car away?" she asked sharply.

"Yes m'am, we did," Kruslov replied.

"Mr. Sewell is going to be very angry."

"I guess so, m'am. You told me he went for a walk. Is that right?"

"Of course it's right or I wouldn't have said so. I don't know what right you have to go into his apartment and take his car away."

"We've got a warrant, m'am. It's legal."

"It may be legal, but it isn't decent. He's a nice young man."

"Mrs. Speers, would you mind if I asked you some more questions about last Sunday?"

"Not at all. But if you think that . . ."

"You said that Mr. Sewell filled up the back end of

his car with trash and took it to the city dump. You mind telling me what he put in his car?"

"Cans and bottles and trash. Why the city can't collect trash the way they do in other places, I'll never . . ."

"I mean, m'am, what were the cans and bottles in? Cartons?"

"There was one carton of trash and then he had a big brown canvas thing packed with trash."

"How big was the canvas thing?"

"Oh, I'd say about as big as a blanket. He had it full of trash and he held it by the four corners, like a sack."

"Did he handle it as if it was heavy?"

"Of course it was heavy! It was full of trash."

"Could the Olan girl's body have been in there?"

I distinctly heard her gasp, and I could imagine the expression on her face. "Why what a ridiculous idea! You must be out of your mind."

"No, lady, I am not out of my mind."

"You must be! Why aren't you out after dangerous criminals, instead of bothering Mr. Sewell?"

"Because I think Mr. Sewell is a dangerous criminal, lady."

"That's incredible!"

Kruslov sighed heavily. Their voices had carried well in the night quiet. I was not more than twenty-five feet from them. The police car radio began to make insane sounds—Donald Duck under a tin wash tub. The patrolman's heels scuffed the gravel as he went quickly over to the car. He spoke a few times in a low voice.

"Nothing yet, sir," he said to Kruslov.

"You are making a dreadful mistake," Mrs. Speers said hotly. Her loyalty touched me.

"We'll see, lady."

"What makes you think he'd do a thing like that?"

I had sensed the growing irritation of Kruslov. Mrs. Speers had a penetrating, indignant voice, and he had had too little sleep. Perhaps under other circumstances he would have kept police business to himself. But Mrs. Speers had refused to be brushed off. He said in a hard voice, "Lady, I do not know what would make him do a thing like that. All I know is we took a look at his car today, at the plant. An expert opened the trunk and he found an empty tin can. There had been frozen orange juice in it. There was a white thread caught where the metal was ragged. The lab boys say that white thread came off the Olan girl's skirt. Now why don't you go back in the house?"

Mrs. Speers was defeated. She left without a word. I was defeated too. I remembered climbing down the slope to get the can. If I'd remembered Mrs. Speers' trash on Monday night, the can would now be in the dump and covered up, white thread and all. Maybe there was a moral there, but I couldn't put my finger on it. I stood in the night behind the tree and felt as naked as the day I was born.

A man carrying a black case came out of my apartment. "You through, Bird?" Kruslov asked.

"I'm through."

Kruslov turned to the patrolman. "You wait in the apartment with the door locked and the lights out. Just because it's dark don't go to sleep. I'll take the car in now. If he's missed by the other cars, you take him when he comes in. Don't take any chances. Cuff him to the radiator and phone in. I'll bet a buck he went to the movies or a bar. If he was still walking, they'd have him."

Kruslov and Bird got in the car and went away. The patrolman stood in the doorway. He took out a cigar, bit the end off and lighted it. He looked at the night for a while and then went into my apartment. The lights went off. I moved slowly back across the side yard, keeping the tree trunk between me and the apartment. There was a high hedge at the far end of the side yard. I wedged myself into it and tried to do some constructive thinking, but my mind wouldn't work. If I turned myself in I would have to try to explain why, after finding the body, I had gotten rid of it. The action seemed to scream of guilt. I kept plaguing myself by asking myself why I'd taken the body away in the first place. It was hardly constructive thought.

Fear grew larger and larger in my mind, fear that I was not going to get out of this. I'd taken her into my apartment and strangled her. I'd driven her car away and abandoned it. I'd come back and slept and disposed of the body the next day. My prints were on her car. Now they'd be looking for the tarp and they'd find it. It seemed to me I'd read that they could type sweat, and my hands had certainly been sweaty when I'd lifted the tarp with her body in it. It had been my belt around her throat, and they'd find that too. I wanted to start running through the night. I wanted to run hard out across the night fields, away from this place.

I thought of everybody I knew, and I could think of only two people in the whole world who would listen to me and believe me. Tory Wylan and Toni MacRae. Tory was far away, but Toni was close.

I moved like a thief through the adjoining back yard. Through a window I saw a woman washing dishes, white dishes with blue rims under hard white fluorescence. I kicked a child's tin toy and scurried into deeper shadows and waited until my heart quieted. I stood by a lilac bush and looked at the lighted windows of the big yellow house. I had an insane wish to throw my head back and yell, "Toni! Toni!" Cry of terror; plea for help. Child in the night.

I circled the big yellow house, all but the front side, staying back far enough so I could see the high windows, but I did not see her. I worked my way back to the original place. I saw her then, in a second story window near the rear of the house. She walked by in front of the window, wearing a yellow robe, both hands fooling with her hair at the back of her dark head. I crouched and felt the ground and found three small stones. The first one rapped off the wood beside her window. The second made a clear sharp clink against the glass. Toni appeared in the window. The light was behind her so that I couldn't see her expression. I threw the last one and it hit the glass, startling her. No one was looking out the other windows. I took my lighter out and held it near my chin and lighted it. The night wind wavered the flame. I put my hand in the area of light and crooked my finger a few times in a beckoning gesture before a stronger puff of wind blew the flame out.

She stood there, not moving. I could guess what was going on in her head: the boss was now reaching for the payoff. I guessed at her anger, yet knew somehow that curiosity would bring her down—and besides, she would want a chance to express indignation. She moved away from the window. When she appeared again she was dressed. She looked down and then left the window. A minute or so later she came walking down through the grass beside the house.

Twenty feet from me she said in a clear voice that seemed audible all over the city, "Mr. Sewell, exactly what do you think you're doing?"

"Hush! Please!" My voice was a frightened croak.

She must have sensed the way I felt. She came close to me and whispered, "What on earth is the trouble?"

"The police are looking for me, Toni. They want to arrest me for the murder of Mary Olan."

"That's simply stupid! You couldn't kill anybody."

"Please, please don't raise your voice like that, Toni. I didn't kill her. But I'll tell you what I did do. I found her body in my closet Sunday morning. I put the body in my car and took it out and left it where they found it. Now they can prove I did that. And if they can prove I did that . . ."

She stood silently in the darkness. "You fool, Clint! You utter damn fool!"

"I know, I know. I did it, I was stupid, I can't take it back."

"You better go right on down there and tell them just what you did."

"You don't know the whole thing. You don't know how bad it looks."

"You can't tell them the truth?"

"I didn't tell them in the beginning. I don't dare to now."

"What do you expect me to do?"

"This sounds silly as hell. I don't know what I expect you to do. I just wanted to tell somebody. I just wanted to tell you. So it's stupid. All right."

She looked down and kicked lightly at the grass. "If you run and hide it'll look even worse."

"I *know* that! But what can I do. I can't keep standing here. I wish I could tell you the whole thing."

"Without any lies? Without leaving out any part of it?"

"I'm off lies, Toni. I've given them up. They don't pay off."

"You ought to go right to the police."

"We can't argue that here."

She turned and looked at the house. There was just enough light from the house for me to see she was biting her underlip.

"I don't want to get you involved," I said.

"Shut up a minute. Have you got your car?"

"They took it away."

"I suppose they're watching your place."

"There's a man in there waiting for me to come home. They think I went out for a walk. They're cruising around looking for me."

"You can come to my room it you do exactly what I tell you to do."

"I don't want to get you involved."

"I am involved. Now listen. There's back stairs. They start from the back hall, outside the kitchen. Take your shoes off."

She handled it like an expert. She went into the kitchen

to create a diversion while I crept partway up the narrow staircase. She left the kitchen and walked noisily up the stairs. As soon as she passed me, I followed in her wake, stepping in her same cadence. I waited at the top, behind the door, while she went down the hall to her room. She opened her room door, looked back toward me and nodded. I moved silently down the hall and slipped into her room. She came in behind me, closed her door and locked it. She crossed the room and closed the blinds at the two windows. I felt weak and shaken. There was one overstuffed chair. I sat in it and lighted a cigarette.

After a few moments I was able to look around the room. It was an ugly room but she had worked hard on it. The high double bed dominated the room. The walls were an unhappy green. Two small lamps with opaque shades muted the ugliness. I could see through the half open door into a small private bath. She had a small corner bookshelf, a wrought iron magazine rack, a double hotplate atop a small cabinet for dishes. It distressed me that the life of Toni should be compressed into this characterless room. I imagined she dated often, she was certainly handsome enough. But there cannot be a date every night. There had to be the alone nights, washing out things, reading, doing her hair and nails, listening to the small coral-plastic radio. The closet door was ajar. Her clothes hung neatly racked, shoes neatly aligned on the floor. She moved over and closed the closet door. The room had a clean smell of her. Fragrant soap, touch of perfume, hint of starch and rustle.

She put an ash tray beside me, moved a straight chair over directly in front of me, and sat there, so close our knees nearly touched. She leaned forward and whispered, "Don't even whisper loudly, Clint. She'd make me move out tonight if she knew I had a man in here."

"All right. I'll tell it from the beginning."

"Not from the time you found her body. From the very, very beginning, the day you met her."

There was a certain avidity in Toni's dark eyes. She

wanted to know all. So I told her all there was to tell.
It took a long time. She would ask questions, not often.
She looked almost sick when I told about getting the
body into the car, about the way it had rolled down the
little hill until the tree stopped it. When I told about the
can and the thread, she said, "I don't understand."

"That was one of the cans I used to disguise the
shape of her in the tarp. When I pushed it down into
the tarp it tore that thread off her skirt. I didn't see it
when I threw the can into the back end of the car."

"Can they prove it came from her skirt?"

"I'm sure they can. They have ways."

We stopped talking as someone walked heavily down
the hall right by her door. She asked a few more questions. She got up restlessly and walked around the room,
touching things absently, straightening them. She sat on
the bed, frowning beyond me. She looked at me and tried
to smile, then blushed and looked away. Her blush under-
lined our nearness, the strangeness of the situation.

I went over and stood looking down at her. "Now do
you think I should turn myself in?"

"I don't know. I don't know."

"While they're looking for me they won't be looking
for who really did it."

"I know, but will they look anyway, after they have
you?"

"I doubt it."

"Somebody killed her, Clint."

"I know that."

"Mr. Raymond?"

"I don't think so. There's too much coldness there,
under all that boyish good nature. Too much calculation.
He wouldn't do anything that stupid. Why should he
kill her? He was perfectly confident that now and then
she would jump into bed with him."

"It's all so . . . nasty," she said, looking up at me.

"Right."

"Clint, I don't think you should turn yourself in yet."

"So what do I do?"

She blushed more violently than before. "You can stay here tonight. Tomorrow I can find out how . . . how convinced they are. Somehow. If they aren't completely sure, then you should go in. If they think they can . . . kill you, then you'll have to go away. I can get you away somehow. I know I can."

It could have been the way she said that. Or the way she looked. Or it could have been a lot of half noticed things adding up in my mind, to make a sudden startling total. Maybe it was merely what she was, and how she was, and who she was. And she was definitely somebody. She was Toni MacRae. She was superbly, uniquely herself. Anyway, it happened to me at that moment. Like, according to the books, it is supposed to happen to everybody.

One minute she was a handsome gal with a good mind, good taste, and far better equipment than average. All that one minute—and then she was suddenly Toni MacRae. Not a pastime, not a hobby, not a target for tonight. Toni. Part of my life. Most of my life. All of my life.

Love at first sight is too trite. When it comes it doesn't creep. It pounces. It isn't even love like I thought of love. It is something else. It is a necessity. It is a place in the road. You get there, turn oblique right, and take a road you never saw before.

She became, all of a sudden, Toni MacRae, indisputable, irreplaceable, unanswerable—as necessary to me as lungs, legs and blood. There is no other way to say it.

I stood there and stared at her. She was miracles. Lips, legs, eyes, breasts. All miracles, all precious.

She was still red. "Just because I say you can stay here doesn't mean that . . ."

"I know."

"What do you mean, you know?"

"All of a sudden, just like that, I know what you mean before you say anything. We could sit without words and carry on whole conversations. Your eyes are wonderful."

"Too loud!" she hissed.

"Sorry." I sat on my heels on the floor so I could look up at her face. I took her hand. She tried to pull it away and then let it rest in mine, unresponsive. "Toni," I said. "Toni!"

"Too loud!"

"Look, it doesn't make any difference if you lock me in your bathroom. Or if I sleep under the bed. One night doesn't matter. We've got us ten thousand coming up."

"Are you out of your mind?"

"I told you, I'm not sure. How can we help not get married, Toni?"

"How can we help . . . what?"

"It's an accomplished fact, anyway. So they stamp a paper for us for the file. Toni, Toni."

She yanked her hand away. "Whatever this is, it isn't funny, Mr. Sewell."

"I know it isn't funny. Toni, I started at the wrong place. I'm disorganized. Let's start at a standard place. I love you."

"Oh sure," she said dubiously.

"All of a sudden. You just sat there, all of you, perfectly miraculous, and it came to me, like it fell on my head."

"This is all just because . . ."

I rocked back on my heels. "Just because I'm going to stay here? It's a fat line. I tell it to all the girls who hide me from the cops. You haven't got any fire around here I can hold my hand in. I've outgrown crossing my heart and spitting. About the only way I can show sincerity is to go trudging out of here. Bake me a cake and bring it to the dungeon. They can't electrocute Sewell. He has to get married. Suddenly I'm confident. Even Kruslov loves me."

I unlocked the door, opened it and started down the hall. She caught my arm with astonishing strength and whirled me around. Her face was like chalk. She got me back into the room, locked the door, leaned against it and closed her eyes. Her color came back slowly. She opened her eyes and looked at me. She looked at me steadily and for a long time. I looked back. I looked back until the room misted out and there was nothing there but her eyes.

She reached me in three small fragile steps. "True?" she whispered.

"True," I said.

She put her hands on my shoulders. I didn't touch her. She put her head a little on the side, still looking, still cautious, still tentative. She put her lips evenly, steadily against mine—firm-soft, warm-cool. All her vulnerability, so sweet you could cry. She was something in my arms. She was a lot of girl. Then she put the side of her dark head against my cheek and we held tight in a drowning world. She shuddered and it went away and she shuddered again and again.

"What's the matter?" I whispered.

"I don't know. So long. . . . The . . . the ice going out, maybe?" She leaned back to give me a crooked grin, but the grin turned into the pinched child-face of tears. She went face down diagonally across the bed, hitting it hard enough to bounce a little. I sat beside her and didn't touch her.

She couldn't possibly feel the same. I sank into a grey swamp—loving and unloved. Then she defeated the tears, turned and curled, and snagged me and hauled me down. This one was a salty kiss. She put the words with it, and the words were fine. It had come true for her some months back and she had been carrying it around, waiting, without much hope.

We lay facing each other, noses touching, her eyes like sooty saucers. When she breathed I took her warm breath deep into my lungs. My hands were on the concave softness of her waist. Her fists lay against my chest. We told each other how wonderful it was. Everything slowly became more heated, crowded, excited. We had started up the slant of a dangerous spiral. I moved away from her.

We whispered until one. We fixed my bed, spare blankets on the floor under the windows, with a sheet and her winter coat over me, and her extra pillow under my head. I was all tucked in in the dark room when she came out of the bathroom, the light behind her. Her summer pajamas might have been hung between two shrubs by a self-respecting spider. She turned out the light and the floor creaked as she came over to me. She knelt and kissed me.

"Sleep well, darling," she breathed against my cheek. She smelled of all the summer gardens of my childhood, with a dash of Pepsodent. I slid my arm around her waist. She pulled back a little.

Then leaning against my arm, she made a funny sound way down deep in her throat and came toward me.

It was a foolish and desperate chance, born of haste and greed. It could have been cheap. It could have spoiled too many things.

But it was magical.

chapter 8

I awakened in the high bed in the morning, awakened early for me, and without any shock of dis- association. I knew exactly where I was and why I was there and all about it. I knew she was behind me.

I rolled over with the greatest of care. The covers were over her shoulder and bunched under her chin. A good clean line went down from the point of her shoulder to the nip of her waist, then mounded up warmly over her hip. A strand of black hair lay across her cheek. Each soft exhalation stirred it. Her face was smooth, faintly dusky, without blemish or scar or mark of living.

The alarm clock behind me let off a horrid clanging. Eyes still closed she lunged for the alarm, sprawling across me. She gave a gasp of fright and shock and yanked herself back, eyes wide and dazed and uncomprehending. I turned and grabbed the metal beast and stilled its fury. When I turned back to look at her, her eyes were shut again.

"Don't look at me," she whispered.

"But I like to look at you."

"Please. I feel so strange."

I kissed her and tried to hold her. She pushed my hands away.

"Go in the bathroom," she whispered.

I took my clothes in, dressed in there. I thought as I walked by the gossamer pajamas, crumpled on the floor near my makeshift bed, that they looked forlorn, be- trayed. After quite a while she tapped on the bathroom

door and I came out. She was in her woolly yellow robe
and her hair was combed. She wouldn't look right at me.

I took her by the shoulders and shook her gently.
"Toni! What's the matter?"

"I . . . I feel ashamed."

I tilted her chin up with my knuckles. "There's no need
for that. Kiss me goodmorning."

She dutifully allowed herself to be kissed. But she still
wouldn't look at me. It wasn't until after she was dressed
that she seemed to regain self-respect.

"Don't make me feel that it was a mistake," I pleaded.

She glowed then. "It wasn't, Clint darling. I know it
wasn't. But . . . well, if you want to know, I never
woke up with a man before. I guess it's stupid. I feel shy
or something. And Clint . . ."

"What?"

"I don't want to do this again until . . . afterward."

"All right."

She looked at me dubiously. "You aren't cross?"

"You're lovely, Toni."

"I've got to go to work."

"Your boss won't be in today."

She stopped the nonsense and gave me my orders:
leave the door locked; not a sound while she was gone;
don't walk, the floor creaks; don't run any water; don't
put the blinds up; don't cough or sneeze; if you snore,
don't take a nap.

"Do I snore?"

She looked away. "I was going to stay awake and sort
of . . . watch over you, but I fell asleep."

She left and the long day began. I heard people moving
around the house, someone using a vacuum cleaner. I
began slowly to starve. I was empty from collar to knees.
I was a hollow tree, with squirrels enlarging the hollow.
As a desperate experiment I ate a Kleenex; it didn't help
a bit. I wished I could risk using the little radio to find out
what they were saying about me. The dull, interminable
minutes went by. I stood at the window and looked out

the crack between blinds and frame and watched the infrequent cars and local delivery trucks go by. Next door an old man, scrawny and withered as a dead chicken, guided an asthmatic power mower back and forth across the May grass.

I thought about my darling. Globe of firm breast, and the flexing satin of haunch. Furnace mouth and cool shoulders. All alive in the whispering darkness, all alive and for me and forever.

And I thought of other women. They seemed poor things in retrospect—flaky skin and sour hair, raddled thigh and suet breast. Not like my darling. Not firm and proud and tall in her skin, like my darling.

He came at three-seventeen. I heard his voice in the hall, suave and easy. "I know this is unusual, Mrs. Timberland, but it's work she brought home from the office and we need it today. She said it would be all right if you'd unlock the door and watch me to make certain I don't steal anything." He laughed and the woman laughed.

A key nibbled metallically at the lock and she said, "I can't seem to get the key in."

"Let me try, will you?"

The key I had left in the door was forced out of the lock. It fell noiselessly to the rug. I came out of my stupor too late to take refuge in the closet. The door swung open and Paul France smiled politely at me. The landlady, a worn woman with a muzzle like a boxer dog, stared at me in shock which turned quickly to outrage.

"What are you doing in my house?" she demanded.

France touched her shoulder gently. "Now, now, Mrs. Timberland. I'll take care of this. I'll see that he's out of your house in five minutes. We can't have this sort of thing, can we?"

He bobbed his head and smiled at her and came into the room and pulled the door shut. She stood out there for a few moments and then went down the hall walking with a very heavy tread.

Still smiling, he said, "A six-state alarm and you hole up two houses away. My goodness." He made a clucking sound with his tongue.

"How did you find me?"

"Your Mr. Wills cooperated with Mr. Pryor and gave me the run of the plant. Including your office. When I began to paw through your desk, the highly decorative young lady became very incensed, too incensed. So I began to look at her more closely. Shall we say she had a fresh high bloom about her? A dewiness? That sort of Joan-of-Arc look young ladies get when they perform a great sacrifice? Once I got her address from your personnel section, I was almost positive. The key on the inside of the door was the clincher, Sewell."

"What do we do now?"

"The fearless investigator takes you in, thus earning his fee."

"Do you think I did it?"

"They think you did."

I moved a little closer to him. I hoped I was being inconspicuous about it. He backed off a little, stopped smiling. "Please don't try anything, Sewell. I can guarantee failure."

I guess he could have guaranteed failure if his luck hadn't been bad and mine hadn't been very good. He made me stand in the doorway, my back to the room. I heard a faint creak and rustle and guessed that he was bending over to pick up the key. I swung my leg back hard. I did it with no anticipation of success, in the mood of a child kicking the wall when he's been stood in a corner. There was a slight shock against my heel and a truly theatrical sound of falling. It was the same sound they use on radio after the ringing shot. I turned around. France lay on his face, his glasses a few feet from his head. Even as I looked at him, he grunted and moved his right arm. I picked up the key, went out in the hall, closed the door and locked it.

Mrs. Timberland was standing down in the hall, her arms folded, chin out. "Tell your friend she has to be out of my house tonight."

I did not answer her. As I went out into the sunshine, I heard France begin to bang on the bedroom door. A grey sedan was parked in front of the house. I threw the room key into the shrubbery.

The world looked different to me. The new and special relationship with Toni had given me a great deal of optimism. False optimism. Up there in the room, with memory so bright and so recent, I had begun to feel that there was good will in the world, that Kruslov would listen, that all could be explained.

But I had left my confidence up in that room. Running down the stairs, I had planned to go turn myself in. That plan evaporated in the sunlight. A woman stared at me from her front porch, then turned and went into her house. I lengthened my stride. If I turned myself in, they would have all they needed. Every bit of it. The joy of a newfound love had affected my judgment. Toni had been brighter about it when she spoke of trying to get me away. I knew that I had to get myself away. I had about twenty dollars on me, a stubble of beard, and the clothes I walked in.

I decided that I would get out of town, somehow. I could contact Tory and he could mail cash to a general delivery address somewhere. I felt as I had in the side lot that night after Yeagger had been knocked out. All the houses had eyes and all the eyes watched me.

I would go far away from them, and later I could get in touch with Toni and she could come to me. I was in panic. My hands were sweaty. I walked as fast as I dared, turning corners not quite at random, heading southeast, knowing that I would hit a main route at the southeast corner of the city. I went through meager neighborhoods, passed candy stores thronged with school children. I turned my face away from traffic, and the impulse to keep glancing behind me was almost ungovernable.

The houses began to thin out. Weeds grew high in vacant lots. Junked cars rusted behind small service garages. Finally I came to the end of a dead end street. The pavement was heaved and cracked. People had dumped rubbish at the end of the street.

I looked south and saw fast truck traffic a quarter mile away and knew that was the highway I was looking for. I cut across lots where the ground was marshy. At one place I had to jump from hummock to hummock. I slipped and went into black mud well over my shoes. I wiped my feet on the grass. Halfway to the highway I came across a young girl and a boy who had made a nest for themselves on a blanket in the tall grasses. After the first glance I did not look toward them. They did not move or make a sound.

At the highway I stopped behind a billboard and tried to regain some confidence. I wanted to crawl into the thick grass and hide there. It was far too easy to think of how they would kill me, quite legally, if they caught me. I walked across the highway, stood on the shoulder and began to thumb the eastbound traffic.

Cars went by at high speed, swirling heated winds around me. Sun glinted off the chrome. Trucks snored by. In between the clumps of traffic, I walked east, keeping my head well down so that traffic headed into the city could not see my face.

I passed a drive-in. Fear had destroyed hunger. Yet even had I been hungry, I could not risk wasting that much time. I kept remembering what France had said about a six-state alarm.

A half mile beyond the drive-in, as I walked, I heard a car coming behind me. I turned with upraised thumb and false smile. It was a highway patrol car. I whirled around, realizing as I did it that my quickness in itself would be cause of suspicion. The car sped by and just as I began to feel better about it, brakes screamed the tires on dry pavement. I saw that it was going to make a U turn as soon as traffic permitted. I turned and leaped the ditch, vaulted a low fence and ran across a cultivated field. As I reached a fringe of woods I looked back. The patrol car was stopped on the shoulder. A man stood by the fence, another near the car. The man by the fence was very still. Something whizzed near my head. A cut leaf circled slowly down. I heard a thin distant cracking sound, and then another.

I dived into the shelter of the woods and ran in terror. I tripped and fell and rolled to my feet and kept running. Branches stung my cheeks. I lost all sense of direction. I knew only that people who wanted to kill me were after me. When I fell the second time it knocked the wind out of me. I lay where I had fallen and listened. I could hear traffic sounds far away. I heard a bird near by, a bird with a fluid intricate call. A jet went over, too high to see, rumbling faintly.

After that I went on more slowly. The woods ended. There was a wide field, a dirt road beyond it. I squatted and watched the road for a time. Nothing came along. I started across the field toward the road. Ten steps from the shelter of the woods, I heard a car coming. I scrambled back. The car stopped a hundred yards down the road and let a man in uniform out. The man stared toward the woods. I knew he couldn't see me, but he seemed to be looking directly at me. I saw him sit on a fence and light a cigarette, still watching the woods.

I moved back until I could no longer see him. I traveled in a line parallel to the road. Soon I came upon another man who waited as patiently as the first. I turned back the way I had come. The woods had seemed vast at first. Now it was a skimpy patch of brush, affording no good place of concealment. It did not take long to find they were on all sides of me. The sun was nearly gone. I knew I could run no longer.

I remembered Toni and I realized I had been in an unthinking panic. France would report where I had hidden.

Toni might be in custody already, charged with aiding me. This was a man hunt, and anyone who had assisted me would suffer.

I came out of the woods at dusk, back by the main highway, my hands held high. Three patrol cars and two Warren police vehicles were there. I was nearly sick with exhaustion. Kruslov was there. They searched me and put me in a car.

Back at police headquarters I was booked, photographed, searched again. They took everything from my pockets, plus my belt and shoelaces and necktie, and put me in a dingy cell. A half hour later I was taken out of the cell and upstairs to a small bare room with barred windows, a spavined conference table, six chairs, a spittoon, a wall clock and another girlie calendar. It was the same set of impossibly lush thighs, but this time a wind, rather than barbed wire, had lifted her skirt.

A young sandy-haired, lantern-jawed patrolman guarded me. He sat on the table and chewed gum and watched me out of colorless eyes. When I asked him for a cigarette, he said he didn't smoke. There was a phone on the corner of the table. A piece of the earpiece had been chipped off.

Fifteen minutes later Kruslov, Hilver, a strange civilian and a male stenographer came in in quick single file, banging the door back against the wall. Kruslov ordered the guard out. They all took chairs. Kruslov put thick hands on his hips and looked down at me.

"Well, damn it, you didn't get very far. Hid out in your girlfriend's room and then tried to hike out of town. Not smart, Sewell."

"Where is she?"

"I ask the questions."

"She didn't have anything to do with it."

"Did you spend the night in her room?"

"That has no bearing on this, Captain."

The back of his hand was like a board. It cut the

inside of my mouth and rocked me so far over I nearly fell off the chair. He smiled, almost genially. "I am going to ask a lot of questions. I want a lot of answers. I have missed a lot of sleep. I am impatient. I do not want smart answers, or a smart attitude. I want a little humility, Sewell. You killed a society girl and you did it very neatly and damn near got away with it. Smart police work caught you. We looked in the trunk of the car of everybody connected with this thing, and in your car we found proof you had her body in there. You ran and you didn't run good enough so you've lost all the way around. You outsmarted Paul France, which is something nobody does very often. That was the last piece of luck you had, the last piece of luck you're going to get. Now I'll ask questions and you answer them. Why did you kill her?"

"I didn't kill her."

He struck me again, in the same place. I wiped my mouth and said, "I want a lawyer."

"You're here for questioning. We haven't placed a formal charge yet. When we place a formal charge, you'll be entitled to an attorney. In the meantime, you can refuse to answer questions. Naturally, we'll have to accept your refusal, but we'll keep asking them. When I'm tired, somebody else will ask them. Where did you kill her?"

"I didn't kill her."

This time I was knocked off the chair. The others watched without any great show of interest.

"You don't want to be stupid about this, Sewell. You see, we can prove you had the body in the back of your car."

"I know I did."

"That's cooperative. Let's have a little more cooperation. If you admit that, then will you admit killing her?"

"But I didn't kill her."

He smiled at me. "I know. The body came in the mail. Special delivery. Or you found it under a bush. Where did you get the body, Sewell?"

"Somebody brought it in in the night and put it in my closet. Mary had a key. I gave it to her so she could wake me up if I was still asleep when she came to get me to go up to the lake Sunday. After your men left I found the body. I was scared. So I got rid of it."

He moved with the bulky quickness of a bear, and all the strength. He lifted me out of the chair with one hand on my throat, swung me around and banged me back against the wall. My head hit hard, dazing me. Through the momentary fog I saw his face wearing a gentle smile, heard his soft voice. "You just found her in your closet. Just like that. Dead."

"Yes," I croaked.

He let go of me, turned with a snort of disgust and sat down again. "Sit down, Sewell."

"It's the truth. She had a belt of mine around her neck. A red fabric belt. It's in the top drawer of my bureau. And I suppose you want the tarp I carried her in. That's in a hole in a rotten birch, about a hundred and fifty feet back in the woods, a hole about seven feet off the ground. I moved the body. I know that was wrong. But I was scared. I didn't think clearly."

Kruslov rattled his fingers on the scarred table top. "Sewell, I'll tell you how it happened. You invited her in. She came in. She was a teaser. She got you all hot and upset and she wouldn't give. You were drunk. You killed her and put her in the closet and went peacefully to sleep."

"How about her car?"

"You drove it out and left it."

"And walked fifteen miles back? Anyway, if I did that, why not take the body along with the car?"

"You were drunk. You didn't know what you were doing." He leaned toward me, smiling softly. "Come on, Clint. We're all men of the world. We know the score. We know how a thing like that can happen. Hell, we know it wasn't premeditated. I'll personally see that you get every break in the world. Honest."

"I didn't kill her. Somebody else killed her and wished the body on me."

He got up and hammered the other side of my face with the back of his hand. It was the sore side. I got my balance and looked up at him. "If you keep your damn hands off me you'll get further."

And he knocked me off the chair.

The civilian interrupted. He was an oily joker with white hair and confidential eyes. "Joe, let me have a minute alone with this boy."

"Okay, Bernie," Kruslov said. They trooped out and left me with Bernie. He gave me a cigarette and lighted it. I fingered the inside of my cheek.

"Son, Captain Kruslov is a good officer, but he's used to handling the lower element. I can see right away that he's not used to dealing with a man like you. But that won't change his methods. He's tireless. He won't give up. He'll give you hell on earth until you come clean with him. Just between the two of us, I think you'd be doing the smart thing to open up. I really do. And he meant it when he said he'd see that you get every break."

"You think I ought to?"

He patted my shoulder. "I'm positive of it. It's pretty sickening the way he cuffs people around. He hasn't injured anybody permanently—yet."

"You can go to hell. I found the body in my closet and that's the entire truth."

Bernie was not like Captain Kruslov; Bernie used the palm of his hand instead of the back. I nailed him right between the eyes, hurting hell out of my hand. He rocked back on the table, legs kicking, and fell off on the other side, taking a chair down with him. Kruslov, Hilver and the stenographer came tearing back in. Bernie wanted me held while he got even. Kruslov told him to sit down and shut up.

We started again. I stuck doggedly to the truth. They kept trying to mix me up. They began to work it in shifts. It is funny what happens to you when people keep driving questions at you, pounding them in, jeering at your answers. You eventually arrive at a semi-hypnotic state. Their heads all looked as big as bushel baskets. Their voices seemed to start inside my head. I no longer knew or cared who asked what. My voice deteriorated to a husky rasp. Somebody started snapping the end of my nose with his finger, every time I answered a question. I don't know when it got dark and the room lights went on. My nose hurt like fire each time it was snapped, but I got too weary to duck. I don't know when the belt and the tarp and the glossy pictures of the body were brought in. I only know that it went on and on and on.

I sat in the bottom of a well with searchlights shining down on me, big heads looking down in there at me. I answered up out of the bottom of my well, my voice hollow. I squatted down there and knew the well was getting deeper and deeper. Their questions were further away. The lights were dimmer.

Suddenly everything stopped. I sat with my chin on my chest. The room was too silent.

"Midnight, Joe," somebody said.

"Yeah," Kruslov said. He yawned mightily. I had trouble establishing which midnight. Wednesday midnight? I remembered that they'd buried Mary Olan this afternoon. It seemed that I had missed the funeral.

"What do you think?"

"Let him cool. We'll try again. Or maybe we won't. There's enough. Principi says there's enough to go ahead on. I'm sick of his damn face. Take him out of here."

They hauled me onto my feet. I felt drunk. Kruslov was by the door. As they started to walk me by him I yanked my right arm free and swung at him. It was a pretty feeble effort. He moved easily away. He looked at me and shook his head and smiled and said, "I'll be damned! Protect me, boys." They walked me out. They had a nice way of getting me down the hall. I couldn't walk at the right speed. They would either prod me in the back, or grab the back of my collar and yank me back. I made it to the dark safety of the grim little cell. It had been there the full hundred years, and it smelled like a flooded cellar.

There was a bare bulb in the narrow corridor. The bar shadows striped the cell and me. I lay sore in the dimness and tried to reconstruct my pride, my oneness, the lost uniqueness of me. In my special innocence I had thought police brutality a thing of myth, of newsstand legend. Oh, they might pound young punks around, beat some humility into street-corner arrogance, slap respect into the weasel-faced, ducktail-haircutted, pimpled little thieves—and it would do them good—but not me. Not Sewell.

Pride in manhood is perhaps a precarious thing. But it is so seldom tested; you so seldom have to lay it on the line. I was a lost child and the big boys had beaten me up in a corner of the school yard. It takes something out of you.

But it puts something back.

I had been somewhat of a wise guy. They couldn't do this to me. I looked back at the last few years—too much pride in my own rightness, in the skills, in the job, in being tall, free, respected and unmarked. Now I was no longer unique. They could reach me. They knew where I lived. It wasn't a big game any more; it wasn't a joke. I realized fully for the first time that a girl was dead, and knew what her death meant. You can't be bright about death. Bright and wise and untouched.

If the heavy hands of Kruslov had done nothing else, they had done one thing. They had awakened me to my own responsibility—the responsibility I had not yet squarely faced. I had to find out who had done it. Her death was my affair.

In a few hours I had done a lot of growing up, most of it overdue. I lay on the thin hard mattress and tried to heal myself by thinking of Toni. But she was far away, and I had not known her. There were other things which had to be done first. Olan money pushed heavily against Kruslov. He had passed the pressure along to me. I was no longer amused.

chapter 9

I spent all day Thursday in the cell. Tasteless food arrived at intervals. There was nothing to read, nothing to hear. It was a quiet place.

Kruslov came as the small high window was turning grey in the May dusk. He came into the cell, rested and amiable, a folded newspaper in his hand.

"Well, boy, the D.A.'s office has approved the file for prosecution and we don't hold you for questioning any more. Now we hold you on a first degree charge."

"What does that mean?"

"They figure they have enough to go on. Now you can have a lawyer. You got enough dough to hire a good one, don't you?"

"I guess so."

"If I was in your shoes, Sewell, I'd want Jerry Hyers. He's tough and he's smart. If you want, I'll give him a ring. He's got a good batting average. Too damn good sometimes."

He puzzled me. He seemed relaxed, friendly.

"I don't know who I want."

"I'm giving you a good steer. Don't look so suspicious. You're not in the killing business. You just got mixed up with the wrong dolly. You'd have had a lot easier time of it last night if you'd talked up."

"Go to hell, Kruslov."

"Okay. Get hard. What's the point? I do my job. It isn't personal with me."

I looked at him and said, as steadily as I could, "I didn't kill that girl."

He laughed. "Come off it, Sewell. Save that for the trial. That's when you'll need it. Shall I phone Jerry?"

"All right. Phone him. I'll talk to him."

"Gosh, thanks!" He tossed the paper on the bunk. "Here, read all about yourself."

I read it after he left. They used a page one picture of me, the picture taken the night I had come home from the police station after getting smacked by Yeagger. I stood looking into the camera with a sickly smile, a perfect picture of guilt.

The write-up was discouraging. The newspaper had tried me and found me guilty. The authorities had certainly not been reticent about leaking their case to the press. They had even figured out how I had worked the car arrangement. According to the paper, we had ridden around until she felt better and then gone back to the club for my car. Driving two cars, we had headed out toward the Pryor farm, getting as far as Highland. Then I had signaled to her to stop. I had overpowered her somehow and brought her back to my apartment in my car. That was the car Mrs. Speers heard driving in at four. I had taken her into the apartment, killed her, taken my car back to the club and walked the two miles back to the apartment. It was fantastic, but it made a frightening kind of sense. Much was made of the belt, the tarp, the juice can, the thread. Nice juicy clues for the reading public.

My first visitor Friday morning was Willy Pryor. He had done some aging since the conference at his home. He looked less like himself in a business suit. He was as brown and hard looking as before, but he did not move the same way. He moved like a much older man. His head trembled a little and his eyes looked sick. It was the damnedest conversation I have ever had with anybody.

"Mr. Pryor, I want you to know that I didn't kill your niece."

"Mary was a wild, reckless girl, Mr. Sewell."

"I didn't kill her."

"After my sister became ill, Myrna and I tried to do our best for Mary. A good Christian home. We taught her right from wrong. But there was the wildness in her. It couldn't be helped, I guess. She was promiscuous, Mr. Sewell. She was evil."

"I wouldn't say that."

"She lived for lust and the gratification of the body. You must know that, Mr. Sewell. You went out with her. You certainly had carnal knowledge of her."

"No. I didn't. In the vernacular, I never got beyond first base. I think you're low-rating her."

He looked at me. There was an Old Testament sternness about him I had not seen before. "Do you deny possessing her, Mr. Sewell?"

"I certainly do. And I didn't kill her."

"She died eternally damned. It was the blood of her father, Mr. Sewell. He was evil. She sinned with many men. I did what I could. I have three young daughters to bring up. She was a bad example in my home, but I was responsible for her. I don't grieve for her, Mr. Sewell. I feel sorry for her. Whoever killed her was acting as the instrument of God."

He was beginning to give me the creeps. "I didn't kill her. I didn't sleep with her. What are you trying to do? Get me to say I did?"

"No, Mr. Sewell." He stood up and looked down at me, thick white brows flaring, nostrils wide. "God have mercy on you."

"Now wait a minute."

"Be of good faith," he said. "Do not despair."

They let him out and he went away.

Jerome B. Hyers came bustling importantly in about ten minutes later. He was a short stocky man in his fifties with a great bulge of forehead and black hair long enough on one side so that he was able to paste it down across his bald pate. He had a mouth as big as a bucket, a ringing baritone voice and small sharp brown eyes. We did not get along at all. Every time I'd explain that I hadn't killed her, Hyers would talk about the privileged conversations a client could have with his lawyer. Then he tried to tell me that the lack of premeditation would make a first degree charge difficult to sustain.

We yelled at each other for a good fifteen minutes. He paced the small cell, with gestures. Suddenly he dropped all his mannerisms. He sat down and took out a big white handkerchief and wiped his mouth and looked at me calmly.

"Didn't do it, eh?"

"No! I've been . . ."

"All right. All right. Let me think. Beautiful circumstantial case. Beautiful! Quarrel at the club. Your belt. Disposal of body."

"I admit getting rid of the body."

He smiled a little sadly. "Young man, I might say that I do not look with great anticipation on basing my case on the assumption that somebody entered your apartment while you were sleeping and put the body in your closet."

"That's what happened!"

"Kindly stop repeating yourself. I accept that. Let me see. May. I'll have until early December to prepare."

"December! Can you get me out of here?"

"There is no bail for a first degree charge. You remain here until then." He looked around the cell and sniffed. He said, "Of course we can see that they make you a good deal more comfortable than this."

"Kruslov and his people knocked me around a lot. Can you make anything out of that?"

"I doubt it. If you had signed a confession we could start thinking about physical duress. But you signed nothing, so we'll just have to forget that. My fee, young man, will be five thousand dollars, plus expenses if I should decide to employ an investigator."

"That's a lot of money."

"I'm a lot of lawyer, young man."

I grinned at him. "Okay."

"I will do some thinking and review the facts we have and come back and bring a tape recorder and we'll go into this in detail, young man."

"What happened to . . . Miss MacRae, my secretary? I'm anxious to keep her out of this."

"That investigator, France, reported where he had found you. Kruslov had her brought in. She was here when they brought you in. Kruslov was willing to be convinced that she had no part at all in the murder. He knows her father, and I guess his brother knows her. He talked to France about it. So the papers didn't get it yet. But I think they will when it comes to trial. The prosecution will want to show that you acted like a guilty man. That includes hiding, and whoever hid you."

"The company will fire her."

He looked at me sadly. "They're not likely to give you a medal, Mr. Sewell."

At about six o'clock they took me to the same room, that shabby defeated room with its smell of violence, where they had roughed me up. Toni was waiting there for me. They closed the door and left us alone. I suspected the influence of Jerry Hyers in that nice arrangement.

We kissed and both talked at once and kissed again. She put gentle fingertips against my swollen face and cried about that, and about us and about the whole miserable mess.

"It can't be true, Clint. It's hideous. It can't really be true."

"Part of it was true."

She flushed. "Yes. Oh, yes. You know, they came to the plant and got me. Captain Kruslov said awful things to me. About helping you. Mr. France was there too. He was terribly angry at you. You chipped one of his teeth. I talked to Mr. France afterward. I asked him if his assignment was over and he said he thought it was. I asked him if he'd work for you. I didn't think he would he was so angry, but he said he would, and I'm going to pay him."

"I don't want you trying to pay his fees."

"I want to. When I run out of money, you can pay him. But I want somebody trying to help you, Clint. Captain Kruslov is so certain it was you that it scares me."

"You know it wasn't."

"Yes. I know, darling."

"Don't ever doubt it. Don't ever wonder about me."

"I couldn't. Don't talk like that." She looked directly at me. "And don't you doubt me. Nothing will ever change. I'll wait for you. I'll work to get you free."

They warned us that we could have but two more minutes together. She said she would be at the office the next morning, Saturday morning, to clean up odds and ends and the phone in my office would be on one of the night circuits if I could get a chance to phone her. She said she would come and see me on Saturday afternoon and bring a change of clothing and toilet articles for me. She had something else to tell me, too, she said, but there wasn't time to explain it. She had to leave then and they took me back to a cell that was colder, barer, more frightening, after the chance I had had to hold my tall warm girl in my arms and hear her voice and look into her eyes. Somebody has to believe in you, all the way. Somebody has to give a damn about you. You have to be important to somebody. Or life is just a routine of going through the motions.

They released me at ten-fifteen on Saturday morning. Hyers stood impatiently while I put the laces back in my shoes, put my belt through the loops, tied my tie around the collar of the dirty shirt. I ripped open the manila envelope, recovered wallet, keys, lighter, change, cigarettes.

"What's up?" I asked Hyers.

"Let's have some coffee down the street."

I was glad it was a small dingy place. With a four day beard and dirty shirt, I looked like a bum. We took a booth near the back of the place.

Jerry Hyers ordered doughnuts and coffee and said to me, "They would have let you stay there all week end. Too damn much trouble to go through the red tape and get you out."

"Would somebody kindly tell me what the hell is going on?"

"Don't you know yet? They found Raymond this morning. Early. A couple of kids were cutting across the Pryor farm, going out on an all day hike. His car was on one of the farm roads. He'd taken his tow rope, climbed up on the roof of the car, heaved the rope over a limb, made it fast, tied it around his neck and swung off the car. The kids couldn't reach the rope even if they'd felt like it. They left him hanging there and ran to the farm. He had the Olan girl's pocketbook in one pocket and the missing key to your apartment in the other. Kruslov got hold of Mrs. Raymond right away. When she found out what had happened she admitted that she had lied about the night when the Olan girl was killed. Apparently Raymond was out until five in the morning. And she told Kruslov that Raymond, as your boss, had fixed you up with dates with the Olan girl so he could see her oftener. She told Kruslov that she was positive her husband had rented a room or apartment somewhere where he could have been seeing the Olan girl. Here's a note. Turn it in at the police garage on Fourth Street and they'll release your car to you. Charges against you have been dropped."

"I thought of Dodd, but I couldn't believe that . . ."

"Nice guy. If his nerve hadn't broken, you'd be holding the big bag, young man. Your check for three hundred will take care of my activities in your behalf."

"I'll mail it Monday."

"Thank you. I have to be off." We shook hands and he hurried out, important and busy.

I finished my coffee, paid the check and found the police garage. After a bored look at the note they told me my car was around in back. Just go down the alley, mister. I drove back to the apartment and phoned my office.

Toni answered, "Mr. Sewell's office."

"This is Mr. Sewell, Miss MacRae. I phoned to tell you I won't be in this morning."

"Clint! Is it true then? There's a rumor around that Mr. Raymond . . ."

"Are there enough people there to cook up a rumor?"

"Clint, tell me and stop fooling. Are you out?"

"I'm out, and you shouldn't be working on Saturday. This is a picnic type day. Where will we go?"

"Clint!"

"Look, darling. I won't be able to pick you up at the plant. I've got to get cleaned up and then I'm going to go see Nancy Raymond. Suppose I pick you up at your place at about two."

"Where are you phoning from?"

"My apartment."

"Well . . . you see, dear, I live there."

"What?"

"Mrs. Timberland threw me out, with harsh words. I had a long talk with Mrs. Speers. That was what I didn't have time to tell you. We thought it would be simpler if . . ."

"Mrs. Speers is knocking on my door right now, it so happens."

"She'll tell you then. I'll see you, dear."

I let Mrs. Speers in. Staring awed at my whiskers, she said, "I heard it over the radio. About Mr. Raymond. I told those stupid . . . ah . . . flatfeet that you hadn't killed that girl. She came from a fine old family, but she was no good. All that drinking."

"I certainly appreciate your attitude."

"It horrifies me to think that anyone would hide a body in my house. Mr. Sewell, I had a long talk with your Miss MacRae. That Timberland biddy threw her out, bag and baggage. We talked about you, Mr. Sewell. She's a splendid girl. We decided that it would be easiest if she would live here while we . . . made every attempt to aid you in your predicament."

"She told me that over the phone."

"Oh, you've talked to her! That makes it easier. I didn't want you to think I'd been too free in letting her use this apartment. Naturally you can't both stay here. I won't have *that* sort of thing going on. You'll have to take a hotel room until she can find other accommodations, Mr. Sewell."

"Yes I . . ."

"You know, I can't help but feel a little disappointed they released you so quickly. Isn't that dreadful of me? I haven't had so much excitement in . . . in just years and years. I imagine you want to get cleaned up after that horrid jail, don't you? Poor Mr. Raymond. She must have driven him insane. Her mother was a lovely person, poor dear. Her father was quite a rounder, though. Remember about that hotel room. Don't forget now!" She wagged a coy finger at me, smirked and backed through the doorway.

I showered, shaved and dressed. I couldn't help having a holiday feeling. It went away when I turned into the Raymond drive and parked near the side door. Mrs. Raymond's heavy old car was there, back from the lake.

The muscular Irish nurse opened the door to me. I said that I wanted to see Mrs. Dodd Raymond. The nurse whispered and took me into a small study to wait. I waited five minutes before Nancy appeared in the doorway. She wore black and she moved like an automaton.

She held a cold hand out to me. "So good of you to stop by, Clint."

"Nancy, I'm terribly sorry."

"Do sit down, won't you? Mother Raymond is taking

this very badly. The doctor left just a little while ago."

"Is there anything I can do?"

"I'd thought of asking you to be one of the pall bearers, but then I decided that under the circumstances we'd better not have any. The funeral will be on Monday at two P.M. The Upmann Funeral Home."

I couldn't get beyond the social glaze. She was saying the formal proper thing.

"Nancy!"

She looked at me and her eyes widened a bit. "I'm all right. I'm really all right. I'm standing it very well, Clint. I made the formal identification of the body this morning at nine. They'll release the body to Upmann some time today after they're through with it."

"You don't act all right."

"I'm perfectly all right. I don't know what you mean. The family burial plot is here in Warren, of course. Mr. Upmann said he would make the necessary arrangements. Mother Raymond wants the Reverend Doctor Lamarr to give the service. I phoned him. He was a little reluctant at first, but he agreed. He said it would be in good taste. Mother Raymond has always been a good friend of the church. I think he thought it would be difficult because the Pryors belong to the same church."

"Nancy, remember me? Clint. I'm your friend. I didn't come to pay the normal sympathy call."

Her face broke and she began to cry. She cried herself to exhaustion. She lay on the leather couch in the small gloomy study and I sat beside the couch and held her hand. It took a long time before she could talk again.

"I hadn't cried before," she said tonelessly.

"It's a good thing to do."

"I was going to go away. I was going to leave him. And he was in trouble. He should have told me."

"He couldn't tell you that."

"I failed him somehow, Clint. I didn't . . . measure up. He wanted more than I had to give."

"He wouldn't find it with Mary Olan."

"I should have guessed something. He's been acting so strangely."

"How?"

"I don't think he slept more than two or three hours the last three nights. Roaming the house at all hours. I tried to call him twice at the office but he wasn't in. He didn't seem interested in the plant any more. He seemed to be thinking something over, making his mind up about something. He wouldn't talk to me. Then yesterday afternoon he talked . . . wildly. I couldn't make any sense out of it. He shouldn't have been home in the middle of the day. He didn't seem to care. His hands were all dirty when he came home. He didn't seem to notice the dirt until I mentioned it. Then he looked at his hands and smiled in a funny way and said, 'Dust of years gone by, darling. Or call it gold dust. That's just as good.' He washed his hands and then came out to the kitchen where I was. He acted as if he'd made up his mind about something. He said, 'I've got it made, baby.' He wouldn't explain what he meant. He had a wild-looking smile. 'C.P.P. can go to hell,' he said. 'We're going to really be in business.' He kept nodding and smiling to himself. He left after dinner. He didn't tell me where he was going. He made a phone call before he left, but I didn't hear who he talked to or what he said. I . . . I won't ever see him alive again."

"Easy, gal."

She looked into space. She held my hand tightly. "It's all over, isn't it?"

"Yes. It's over, Nancy."

She turned her face away from me. "I keep thinking of something awful," she said in a small voice.

"Like what?"

"Like waiting until this is all over. Six months. Or a year even. And then going back and finding a way to have the good years."

"What do you mean?"

She turned abruptly toward me, her eyes almost fierce. "We must be almost the same age, Clint. I'd know how to be good for you, in the job and everything. I know the life. We had tests, you know. It wasn't me, I can have children. It would be right this time. Young people all living together. And transfers to new places. I know it all. You could be proud of me, people like me. I was always active on committees and things. I made every new place look good. It was all good until we came here. That's the horrid thing I keep thinking."

I didn't say anything and I didn't release her hand. She turned her face away again.

"Stupid, wasn't it?" she said.

"You're upset."

"It isn't you. I just want that way of living back. I just want to be like that again, only this time with children. I'm sorry, Clint."

"Don't be sorry."

"You wouldn't try it, would you?"

"I'm sorry."

She took her hand away. I stood up and said goodby to her. She didn't move or answer or look at me. I let myself out. Just as I reached my car, Kruslov drove in. He and another man started toward the house. I cut over and intercepted them.

"Now what?" Kruslov asked. He looked square and dull and tired.

"Now I want to know how proud you are, Kruslov. I want to know how big a charge you got out of slapping me around."

He eyed me coldly. "Want an apology?"

"You might try one for size."

"Never, you damn fool. You found a body and moved it. What the hell right has a civilian like you got meddling in police work? You complicate my job, mess up the evidence, shoot off your mouth and then come prancing around looking for an apology. There's statutes that cover what you did, and if I get too damn annoyed at you I may see if I can make some of them stick. Now get the hell out of my way."

I got out of his way before he bounced me out of his way with a heavy shoulder. He went on into the house. I felt like a spanked child. I got into my Merc and drove away.

I had won my argument with Toni and moved some of my stuff into a second class hotel room. I won it by telling her that if I knew C.P.P., I wouldn't remain in my job for more than another few days. We had taken a bag of cheese and liverwurst sandwiches and a cold six-pack of beer far into the country. Before we left, I had brushed off two reporters with more dispatch than finesse.

From the grassy bank we could toss crumbs into the river. Minnows struck the crumbs ferociously. I lay back and her slack-clad thigh fitted the nape of my neck as though designed for that special purpose.

"Stop frowning," she said softly.

"Can't help it."

"It's all over now."

"A cold guy, Toni. A type who figured all the angles. A ruthless guy. Could he kill? Yes, if it would give him a big gain, and if he was logically certain he could get away with it. Would he kill himself? Perhaps, if he was aware that he would be caught. So how does it fit? Not at all. No gain in Mary's death. And he wasn't about to be caught."

"In the immortal words of the bard, leave it lay."

"Can't."

"Maybe it's all different than it looks, Clint dear. So what? We're out of it. You don't *owe* anybody anything. Now we just think of us."

"Female reasoning. Ten thousand years ago you'd have your own lady-weight club leaning against the cave wall, just inside the door. And uninvited guests—boom."

"And ten thousand years ago you'd be seeing how close you could get to a saber-toothed tiger. Hah! Male reasoning."

"But I can't let go of it, girl. The package is too neatly

wrapped. The string is too carefully tied. Maybe too carefully tied around Dodd's throat."

"Don't!"

"I'm not in love with his memory. I've got no yen to
vindicate him. Good sense says to do as you suggest.
Leave it lay. And spend a lot of the tag ends of the hours
of my life wondering."

She ran a gentle thumb along one of my eyebrows and
then the other. She sighed heavily. "Meddler."

"I know."

"Big fool."

"I know that too."

"If you gotta, you gotta."

"Mmmm. You are a special deal, MacRae."

"The large economy size deal."

"Three dimensional, color, bite-sized, built-in flavor."

We kissed until the river ran uphill. The minnows gog-
gled at us. All the trees applauded, and a brown and
white cow strolled down to the river edge to watch with
benign gravity. We gave her a spare sandwich. She ate it
with the dignity of a baroness. Then we went back to
the car. She took hold of my arm. Her fingers bit in. Her
dark eyes spotwelded my soul.

"Be careful," she said.

Yes, I would be careful. But it was something I had to
do. I had to know. They had changed me—Kruslov and
his hands, the damp cell, the dead girl. Before I had
changed I could have said that it was none of my business. But I had changed and become more involved with
life. As with John Donne and his talk of no man being
an island.

Death had come very close to me, black gauze wings
grazing my face. I could not tell myself it was all over.
Not while I had these nagging doubts. I could not let Dodd
Raymond be buried with that mark on him.

And I would be careful. Because afterward, there
would be Toni.

chapter 10

There are few places where a man can dirty his hands with the dust of the past. After I left Toni off—a rather disconsolate but understanding girl—I went to the Warren Public Library. It was the same vintage as the police station. The young lady who came to my assistance wore a white angora sweater that struggled to contain two of the most enormously unreal breasts I have ever seen. She marched trimly behind them, using them as weapons of offense. I wondered how anybody ever remembered what question they had come to ask. They had a life of their own—mammalian, incredible—objects far beyond the realm of desire, creating only awe and consternation.

I managed to stammer my question about old records and newspapers. She pointed toward a side stairway with those breasts and said that they had booths up there and micro-film projectors and a girl who would help me. I went up the stairway.

The upstairs girl was of different construction. Between the two of them they had two sets of normal equipment. She explained the setup to me and told me that if I knew what I wanted, she would get the rolls and I could sign for them. I told her I didn't know what I wanted. I told her I wanted to see any rolls a Mr. Dodd Raymond had looked at yesterday afternoon. She became skeptical and uncooperative. She had heard about Mr. Raymond and had recognized the name at once. I confessed that I was not with the police. Finally she allowed as how she could look at the records and tell me. She came back from her desk in a few minutes and, with a relieved icy smile, told me that Mr. Raymond had not signed for anything. It was what I expected. Miss Ice kept her domain spotless.

I thanked her and went back down the stairs and out— not without trying for a last look at Miss Angora. She had disappeared.

The *Ledger* Building was a three story oblong, quite new, of tan stone and aluminum. A quote about freedom of the press was lettered in bronze beside the main door. I got there a few minutes after five. The business end of the paper, the people with regular hours, were leaving. Trucks were swinging out of the side alley with the after- noon final.

A girl behind the classified counter on the main floor stopped applying raspberry lipstick long enough to tell me, with calculated insolence, that it was late and maybe I could find what I wanted on the second floor.

The file of bound editions was in a small room next to the morgue. A bouncy, swarthy little girl with rhinestones set into her glasses frames looked at me carefully and told me I could help myself.

"Do you keep any record of who uses these?"

"Oh no. Nobody uses them very much any more except the news staff sometimes. The public library has them on micro-film going all the way back to 1822 when the *Ledger* first started to come out as a weekly. Why don't you use theirs? They're handier and cleaner."

"Well, as long as I'm here."

"That's okay. Handle the old ones carefully, won't you? They're pretty brittle."

"I'll be careful."

She left me in the small room. One set of bound copies covered one wall of the room, with boards locked across the fronts of the volumes so they could not be taken out; another set was unconfined. I had to find out which volume Dodd Raymond had been interested in—if my guess was right. I found the switch that controlled the overhead light and moved close to the books. The recent years' copies were quite free of dust. I ranged back over the years. One volume stood out, most of the dust gone from the spine. I slid it out and carried it over to the table.

Just as I set it down two men came in, so involved in a heated argument about the Giants that they barely glanced at me. They picked one of the recent volumes, spread it out, turned the pages with silent intensity. Then one pointed with his thumb and said, "Hah!"

"So okay. So I was wrong."

"So you buy."

They put the book back and left. I began to go through my volume. The paper was yellowed, the corners brittle, the type face more quaint than in the current editions.

A half hour later and two-thirds of the way through the volume, I found it. I read it carefully. It had warranted quite a splash in the paper.

I read it and read the follow-up stories in subsequent editions. The last little flicker was a page eight squib telling about the transfer of Mrs. Rolph Olan from a local hospital to a private mental institution in accordance with a court order.

I sat back and pulled the peanut-can ash tray closer and lighted a cigarette. It was not a pretty story. Mary Olan, on an October Wednesday, had been picked up at two-thirty at the private elementary school she attended by the Olan chauffeur driving Mrs. Olan's car. The little girl had run into the house. She had seen her father's car in the drive and was anxious to see him. Her baby brother was having his nap. The cook and maid had Wednesday afternoons off. She went in the front door. Her mother, Nadine Pryor Olan, was standing on the bottom stair of the main staircase. She held a bloody kitchen knife in her hand. Her husband was on his back on the floor in front of her, stabbed through the heart and quite dead. Nadine Olan was in a state of severe shock, unable to respond to questions.

It was established—though the paper was most coy about this—that Rolph Olan had led an active extra-marital life and that this had been a cause of discord between them. Except for the sleeping child, they had been alone in the house. They were unable to establish why Mr. Rolph Olan had come home in the middle of the day. He had received a phone call at his office shortly before he left and it was believed that it was his wife who had called him home, though this could not be proved. He had a habit of answering his own phone, perhaps due to his concurrent intrigues.

At first Nadine Olan, whose health had always been delicate, had responded to treatment. She claimed that she had heard a fall shortly after she had heard her husband's car drive in. She said she had been resting in her bedroom next to the nursery. She had thought little of it, had called to her husband, and then begun to worry when he didn't answer. She had gone down and found him and she guessed she had instinctively pulled the knife from his chest. The next thing she knew, her daughter had come running in and had started to scream.

She had been quite calm for a few days and then, perhaps as she began to realize that everyone was quite certain she had killed him, her mind failed quickly. I guessed that it could have been due to her own uncertainty as to whether or not she had killed him. Faced with such an insoluble problem, a retreat into unreality would not be inexplicable, particularly in the case of an emotional, sensitive, unhappy woman.

During Mrs. Olan's period of relative calmness, the paper speculated about two facts which seemed to spoil the picture of guilt. One man, who knew Rolph Olan by sight, was almost willing to swear that he had seen another man riding homeward with Mr. Olan that afternoon. And a neighbor woman reported that on that same afternoon a man had cut across her grounds and could have been coming from the Olan residence.

But when Mrs. Olan's mind went, before she moved

back into the silent darkness where she could not be reached, she made a confession of sorts. Portions of it were reprinted in the paper. It was wildly incoherent. It spoke of angels of death and the vengeance of the Lord. It spoke of sin and retribution. Her obvious insanity put a halt to further speculations about her innocence.

During the days immediately following the murder, Mr. Willis Pryor, brother of the accused woman, spent countless hours by her side, even watching over her during the night, and was tireless in proclaiming her innocence. He wrote a letter to the paper criticizing the inertia of the police. After Nadine Olan's collapse and the medical verdict that the prognosis was unfavorable, Willis Pryor ceased his efforts in her behalf, withdrew from many community activities and resigned from the boards of several local corporations.

I sifted over what I had. It wasn't much. It was certainly less than Dodd Raymond had. He had known enough to kill him. This was his town; he'd know little things that hadn't been in the paper. He had perhaps used the paper to confirm his memories. And he had known Mary Olan well. She would have talked to him about such things, though not to me.

All I had was a hunch. A hunch about the evil of righteousness.

I took Toni out to dinner that Saturday evening. I guess I was poor company. I would join our group of two for a while and be fine. And then I would drift away again. Toni was aware of it, and she was half amused, half hurt. I did as well as I could, returned her to my apartment and holed up at the hotel. I phoned her after I was in bed with the light out. I could picture her sitting by my phone. She said she was wearing another pair of those delightfully diaphanous pajamas, and that she too was in darkness.

We said the things you would expect to be said under such circumstances and it was all very very fine indeed.

Two hours later, nightmare yanked me out of dreams.

I felt as exposed and afraid and naked as if I had been flayed. The object of fear was gone; I couldn't remember it. I could only remember running in slow motion with something coming after me that moved faster and faster.

The Pryor farm was, in its own way, as much a showplace as the house. Fat black cattle grazed on juicy grasses behind bone white fences. The aluminum roofs of the cattle barns blazed in the Sunday morning sun. I slowed down to watch a pack of horses running like hell. No reason. They felt good. It was that kind of a morning. Two big fieldstone posts marked off the entrance. The gravel road led straight from the entrance to the tenant house. Beyond the house, on the gentle slope of a hill, were the two cottages where the Pryors stayed when they stayed over at the farm. The cluster of barns and silos was behind the tenant house.

I ignored the severe private signs and drove on in and parked by the tenant house. A new red tractor stood in rigid angular dignity, like a strange Martian insect.

John Fidd came around from behind the tenant house and looked at me with disgust. "Yar?" he said.

"Came back down from the lake, eh?"

"No horses and no boats up there this summer. On account of Miss Mary. And that no good Yeagger. Good thing. I got too much to do here without going up there and being a stable boy. I got to watch the hands here."

"I'd like to see the place where they found Mr. Raymond yesterday morning."

John Fidd spat with emphasis. "Wouldn't be anybody driving around the place at night if I was here. I can't show you now. Too busy."

"How do I find it?"

"You don't," he said.

That seemed to be that. He looked beyond me. A yellow jeep swung into the gravel road, rear wheels skidding dangerously. It was piloted by one of the Pryor girls.

"Which one is that?" I asked.

"That there is Miss Skeeter, the oldest. Best of the lot, too, if anybody should want to ask me."

She stopped beside my car and jumped out of the jeep. She wore beat-up khaki riding pants, a yellow sports shirt. Her brown hair had paler sun streaks. She looked as round, brown, healthy and uncomplicated as a young koala bear. "Hi, John. Hello, Mr. Sewell. John, I thought I'd give Simpy a run."

"You're out early, Miss Skeeter."

"I went to church early. The rest were about ready to go by the time I got back to change. Dad will probably bring the rest of them out later on."

"Mr. Sewell here was wanting to see where that fella hanged himself. I don't have the time right now to take him over there."

She looked at me dubiously. "If you really want to see it, I'll show you where it is. Wait until I saddle up and then you can follow me in the jeep. Or maybe you'd like to ride too?"

"No thanks. The jeep will be fine."

She trotted off toward the barns. I leaned against the jeep. Fidd went off. In about five minutes she came out on a big roan that was all stallion and half as high as a house. He felt like going sideways. She yanked some sense into him, touched him with a little crop and cantered up to the jeep.

"Once we get beyond that fence line there we'll cut across country. Better put it in four wheel drive. Do you know how?"

"Yes."

"Don't follow Simpy too close. He gets nervous."

She spun him and lifted him into a full run. There wasn't any danger of my getting too close. I had enough trouble keeping him in sight. Far ahead of me she cut over toward a dirt road and swung to the ground. The far side of the road was lined with trees. I drove up and stopped and got out.

"This is the tree and that's the limb there. See, he had the car right about here, so that the limb was about ten feet above the roof of the car and about five feet behind it. It was easy to throw the rope over the limb."

"I wonder why he came out here?"

"They say he used to come out here a lot years ago. They used to ride out here. He didn't really date Mary then. She was too young I guess."

Simpy cropped grass steadily. Skeeter seemed anxious to get on him and be off. I wanted to get her talking, and I didn't know exactly how to go about it.

"I guess they had to get a ladder to cut him down."

"I guess so."

"How do you feel about it, Skeeter?"

"What do you mean?"

"About Mary and Dodd Raymond."

"I didn't know him very well. Just to say hello to. I'm certainly not sorry he's dead, Mr. Sewell. Everything seems so dull without Mary. She was wonderful. We loved her, my sisters and I. It was a terrible thing to do."

"I guess it was, all right."

"Simpy wants his run. You can leave the jeep back by the house."

"How old are you, Skeeter?"

"Seventeen."

"The last time I saw you was a week ago today."

Her eyes seemed to change to a paler color. "I know. When you came up to the lake after throwing Mary's body out in the bushes, acting up there like nothing had happened. I remember it very well, Mr. Sewell."

"That was a mistake. It was bad judgment. I lost my head."

"You looked calm enough up at the lake."

"Skeeter, I was scared to death. Honestly."

She weighed that carefully. "I guess maybe you had every right to be. But you did a bad thing."

"I know that. I had that impressed on me . . . forcibly."

"She was so alive."

"I know." I braced myself carefully, smiled and said, "A little too lively for her Uncle Willy, I guess."

"I don't think I know what you mean," she said with young dignity, slamming the family gates.

"From things she told me, I gathered that your father didn't care much for the way she led her life."

"Mary told you that?"

"We talked a lot. Remember, I knew her pretty well, Skeeter."

"Have you got a cigarette? I'm not allowed to smoke, so I can't carry them."

I gave her a cigarette, lighted hers and my own. She hitched her tight pants onto the flat surface of the front fender of the jeep. "She just about drove Daddy crazy. He's awfully strict with us. He tried to be the same way with Mary, but it didn't work because she was of age and had her own money. There wasn't any way he could punish her or restrict her the way he does us.

"At Christmastime Daddy caught Jigger kissing a boy. Just kissing a boy! You'd think she was living in sin or something. Jigger didn't get any allowance and she couldn't have a date or even go to the movies for six whole weeks. After dinner she had to go right to her room and study until bedtime. And he restricted Dusty and me for two weeks because he'd caught Jigger. Honestly!"

"They must have fought then?"

"If you can call it fighting. Daddy was either yelling at her or not speaking to her. She never seemed to get mad. She acted as if it was some kind of a joke. I couldn't ever figure out why she didn't go and live alone where she could do as she pleased and Daddy wouldn't know anything about it. That's what I would have done. That's what I will do, the minute I'm old enough. It sometimes seemed to me that she stayed with us just to needle Daddy. I think there was some legal reason why he

had to provide a home for her for as long as she wanted
it."

"She needled him?"

"I don't know exactly how she'd do it, but she could
sure raise hell with him. When he'd be having one of his
bad spells over something she had done, or something
he thought she'd done, she would find a chance to say
something to him. She'd never let any of the rest of us
hear what she said. It must have really been something,
though. Sometimes Daddy would go and walk for hours
after that happened. Or lock himself in his study and we
could hear him in there reading the Bible out loud. You
know I've always thought she . . . she told him about
. . . men."

She was blushing under her tan. "What?" I said.

"About men. Because Daddy has told me, gosh, dozens
of times, not to let Mary talk dirty to me, and come and
tell him right away if she did. She never did, of course.
But that's the way I think she must have talked to him.
Daddy is strong and he has a terrible temper sometimes.
Like the time he broke Dusty's arm when . . ." She
stopped abruptly. "That's none of your business. I
shouldn't have said it."

"You've said most of it. Maybe it would sound better
if you explained it."

"Actually she fell."

"Pushed?"

"Well, yes. But he didn't *mean* to break her arm. I
guess I better tell you. I still don't understand it. It was
two years ago. Mary had come home from a trip. It was a
warm day in early October and we went up to the lake,
the six of us. I guess Dusty thought Daddy and Mother
were up at the big house. Jigger and I were still in the
water. Mary had gone to the girl's shower room over the
boat house. Dusty decided to sneak up into the men's
bunk room and look at some cartoons on the wall up
there. We're not supposed to look at them or even know
they're there. They aren't really dirty, just kind of silly."

"I've seen them."

"Dusty sneaked up and Daddy was up there at the window with a pair of binoculars looking over toward the girls' bunk room. He got angry and chased Dusty down the stairs and pushed her. She fell and broke her arm. She didn't tell us about the binoculars until later. He could have been trying to see Mary get dressed, but that doesn't make much sense. He'd hate anything like that. I've just never been able to figure out what he was doing. I even asked Mary about it one time. She looked startled and then she laughed and laughed. Tears ran down her cheeks she laughed so hard. She wouldn't tell me what was so funny. At dinner that night she looked at Daddy and started laughing all over again. He got so mad he couldn't eat. He left the table."

I had almost all of it. Nearly everything I needed. The pattern was all too clear. I looked at the snub-nosed healthy girl and pitied her. But maybe she and her sisters would have the strength they would need. Maybe the blood of Myrna was strong enough, clear enough, sane enough. Yet probably nothing would ever keep this girl from hating me.

"It must be pretty tough on your father, with what happened to his sister, and now what's happened to his niece. I understand your father and his sister were very close."

"They were only a year apart. They were inseparable when they were young. I think he nearly died when they had to send her away. I was just a baby, of course. Mother still talks about how sick he was."

"He looks pretty husky now."

"Oh yes. He's *very* healthy for a man his age. Do you know what he did last fall? All by himself, with an axe, a handsaw, a sledge and wedges, he cut down trees and sawed them up and split over fourteen cords of hardwood. There was so much more than we needed that John Fidd sold six cords in town for twelve dollars a cord."

"He works out here a lot, I guess."

"Oh, yes."

I braced myself again and made it casual. "I suppose he was working here the last time I saw you up at the lake. Was your mother along?"

"Let me think. Yes, she was up there with us but went back early when Daddy phoned about Mary. Daddy doesn't like us to go up alone, even though Mrs. Johannssen and Ruth are there. Mother isn't as strict with us. Daddy stayed in town. I don't know whether he stayed home or out here. Maybe here."

"And nobody went up this weekend."

"No, we all stayed in town."

"Did your father stay out here Friday night?"

"No. He was out here on Friday, but he came home . . . why are you asking me that?"

"Just making conversation, I guess."

She was looking dubious again. I made my smile as bland as possible. "You certainly stick to that horse nicely. He'd scare me."

She slid off the fender. "He's an old lamb. He's a honey pie, old Simpy is."

She caught him, mounted, waved and rode off. His hooves drummed the May earth. I looked at the tree. Dodd Raymond had hung there, night dew on his shoulders, on the wavy hair, two hundred pounds at the end of a tow rope, while dawn came and the birds awakened.

I drove the jeep back the way I had come, following my tire tracks in the pasture grass.

As Toni would say, it was none of my business. But you can't leave a thing like that alone. Not when you're nearly positive.

I waited a full hour before they arrived—Uncle Willy, Aunt Myrna and the other two girls. Skeeter came cantering back to the barn just as their car drove in. The girls got out, gave me a quick unconcerned glance and raced toward the barn. Willy halted them with one short bark. They came back meekly, took the two baskets of food and carried them toward one of the cottages. Myrna Pryor stared at me and followed the girls.

Willy came over toward me. His polished boots gleamed black in the sun. His riding pants were crisp and fresh. His white shirt was unbuttoned, the tails knotted at the waist à la Mexican beach. His hair was almost impossibly white against the tan of him. He was a Hemingway, fifty, taut as drums, resilient, proud of his body.

"Hello, Sewell. Something I can do for you?"

The look of defeat he had worn in the jail cell was entirely gone. His eyes were clear, keen.

"Your eldest has been showing me the tree where Dodd was found."

He frowned a little. "Did you arrange to meet her here, sir?"

"No. No. I just happened to get here at about the same time. Lovely girl."

His face was unfriendly. "Yes, she is."

"You have three fine daughters, Mr. Pryor."

"Did you come out here to tell me that, Sewell? I might say that I have no particular urge to entertain the . . . companions of my late niece. It's over and I want my daughters to forget about it as soon as possible. The whole thing was sordid and unfortunate."

"Yes, it was."

"Now if you wouldn't mind leaving, we're having a family picnic here today."

"Under the same tree?"

He stared at me. "If that's humor, Sewell, I find it a little strange. If it isn't humor, you should know that I'm physically capable of throwing you into your automobile."

"I guess you are, at that."

"Please go, will you?"

"I want to talk to you."

"There's nothing I can conceive of that we can talk about."

"I just wondered if another man could take over that

business opportunity Dodd mentioned to you, Mr. Pryor."

He stood there, the sun on his face, looking at me, fists on his hips, brown arms flexed. I cannot say there was any physical change. I saw no change. But I sensed a change that went on inside. I sensed a shifting, a re-evaluation, a new poise of forces. A man might sit at a poker table with that same immobility, certain from the restrained betting that his was the winning hand, and then see a large bet made.

"I'm not sure I know what you're talking about."

"Dodd was going to speak to you. He told me he was. I understand you were going to finance him."

"I'm not interested in new business ventures."

"He said you were interested in his."

"Then he lied to you, because I never heard any proposition from him. I thought he was satisfied with his job."

"Maybe I should rephrase it. He said you couldn't *help* but be interested in his proposition."

"That's a strange statement."

"Isn't it."

"Are you trying to be cryptic? You're talking way over my head, young man."

"I don't imagine it was the money that stopped you. I guess it was just having someone know. Or maybe you have that strange form of distorted honesty that saw it as one way to get me out of a jail where I didn't belong. There was a good chance I might get electrocuted for killing her. You wouldn't have liked that. Conscience is a funny thing, Mr. Pryor. Even your twisted one."

"This is the damnedest nonsense I ever heard."

I measured the distance between us and then said softly, "How did she look through the binoculars, Willy? Lush and desirable? You know when I mean. When you broke Dusty's arm."

"You must be quite mad." He said it with discouraging calm.

"It's the hot sun, Willy. I wonder how you fit your conscience around another thing, though—that elastic conscience of yours. How . . ."

"Why don't you leave before I throw you off my land?"

"How do you adjust to what happened to your sister? You did that, you know. You killed the father and then watched the father's blood come out in the daughter. You framed the beloved sister Nadine."

Again it was the poker table. He had matched the large bet. Now the stranger's cards were turned over. He looked beyond me. His mouth moved and was still. His eyes saw nothing.

"There'll be more," I said. "Somebody else will figure it out next. Maybe one of your own girls. Maybe your wife. Or maybe she half suspects already. There aren't any secrets, Mr. Pryor. Not about a thing like this."

There was something reminiscent of a bull in the set of his shoulders, in the hump of muscle at the nape of his neck. He came at me with the wild sudden fury of a bull. I had driven him a little bit too far. There was no room in his brain for cold plans and projects. There was room for nothing but fury, a very desperate fury.

I had destroyed his world and I must in turn be destroyed. A fist like a sledge numbed my left arm. I struck back once and a second blow thumped my ribs and he was on me. His arms locked around me, head driving against my chin, knuckles in the small of my back. I tripped and fell heavily and he was on top of me, smashing the wind out of me as he fell. I was young and reasonably husky, but you can't fight that sort of fury. You can't even survive that kind of fury. He got a blocky knee on my stomach and husky brown hands locked around my throat. I tensed my throat muscles and tried to get hold of a finger to pry it back and loosen his grip. My hands were sweaty and I could not get a grip. The last bit of air rasped in my throat and then his hands closed the air passage. My chest convulsed. The sun swam and darkened and I slapped weakly at his face with hands made of balsa and paper, like the frail drifting wings of toy gliders.

He was taken off me. I sat up, retching and coughing, and color came back into the world. I saw Pryor stagger and then make what must have been a second or third charge at Paul France, trying to get his hands on him. He hit Pryor three times as Pryor came at him, moved almost casually to the side and hit him twice more as Pryor went by. The last blow was decisive. Pryor's legs worked for three more strides before he went down on his face. The four Pryor females came running down from the cottage, one of them emitting short sharp screams with each stride. John Fidd appeared with a shotgun.

I got to my feet. A lot of little white dots whirred around like so many bees and slowly faded away. France said, "Your girl said to find you and keep an eye on you, bub."

"Thanks."

He touched a red mark on his chin and said, speculatively, "Think nothing of it. Nothing at all."

"Get back," Fidd snarled. "Get back against that car, both of you."

France walked directly toward him, took the shotgun, wrenched it away from him, murmuring softly, "Easy, Dad. Easy now."

The girls had rolled their father over onto his back. Mrs. Pryor was demanding to know what had happened.

I said to France, "I've heard a citizen can arrest another citizen. Is that the truth?"

"It's legal. What have you got on him?"

"He murdered Rolph Olan, Mary Olan and Dodd Raymond."

Skeeter flew at me like a fat brown robin—a robin with claws. "That's a damn lie!" she screamed. "You're a big liar!"

Willy Pryor hadn't opened his eyes or moved. He opened his mouth and said, "It isn't a lie. It's the truth." He got up slowly and steadily, brushed his women aside and walked toward us. "Which car do you want me in?"

France opened the door of his grey sedan. "Right in here, please."

I followed the grey car. The Pryor car, with the four females and John Fidd, followed me. It was a bright Sunday and seventeen miles to Warren, with the first part of it through lovely farmland. We went by with our load of heartbreak. The cows didn't care. The bees didn't care. The birds didn't give a damn. It was May with summer coming up.

Kruslov let me sit in on it. He acted like a man who had been hit sharply over the head. He kept staring at Pryor and shaking his head, almost imperceptibly. It was Sunday and it took a little time to gather the official cast.

Willis Pryor sat stolidly, dominating the small room with a sort of sad force and dignity, waiting, motionless, grave. He seemed like the chairman of the board awaiting tardy members with iron patience.

The pasty-faced stenographer uncapped a huge prehistoric fountain pen of a peculiarly poisonous shade of orange. I sat where I could see dark bruises on the left side of Willis Pryor's jaw.

"I guess we're ready, Mr. Pryor," Kruslov said apologetically.

"Shall I tell this all as it happened?"

"Please, sir."

"My sister Nadine married Rolph Olan. Shortly after marriage he began to make her life a hell on earth. She confided in me, we were always close. I spoke to Rolph several times during the years. He ignored me. He seemed amused by me. His infidelities were becoming notorious. It was no life for my sister. On the day of his death I phoned him at his office. I said I had to speak to him. I insisted. I had prayed for guidance. I wanted to give him one last chance. He picked me up on the corner I mentioned. I said we could talk at his house. I hoped to bring Nadine into the conversation. Nadine was resting. We talked quietly in the study. He told me that Nadine was as tasteless to him as weak tea. He said he would not spend his life chained to the living dead. He said he had decided to divorce her. That was his answer. I excused myself saying I wanted to get a drink of water. I brought the knife back from the kitchen. He had gone into the front hall, to go up the stairs and wake her and tell her his decision. I struck him with the knife. He looked down at it and raised his hand and touched the handle and tried to say something and fell. I went out through the back of the house.

"It never occurred to me that Nadine would be suspected. I hoped the police would suspect some prowler, or some business enemy. After her mind started to go, I told her that I had done it. I told her why. I couldn't reach her, she didn't understand what I was saying. I had done that to her. Once I knew she was incurable there seemed little point in confessing. I had my own wife to think about, an infant daughter, another child on the way. I contemplated suicide. I was mentally sick and physically sick for a long time. Eventually I recovered. Had it not been for Rolph's evil actions, Nadine would not have lost her mind. Once I had decided that, I was able to regain my physical and mental health."

He was silent for a long time. Kruslov stirred in his chair but did not speak. Pryor's face was still, and he was far away in old memories.

Pryor looked up with a little start. "Rolph's death and Nadine's collapse left me with the responsibility for the school child, Mary, and the infant, John. I had never had any trouble with John. He is brilliant, devious, and of a metaphysical turn of mind. But his mind is stronger than his body. He has never evidenced the weaknesses of the flesh. Mary was a different problem. I have thought about her a great deal. She was born old. She was born with a knowledge of evil. Often as I beat her, I could never subdue the evil in her. Once she became of age and began to receive her own income, I no longer had any hold over her. She hated me. She hated me because of the punishments I had inflicted for her own good. With the devilish wisdom of her black heart, she began to punish me in turn. She decided to debauch me and my daughters.

"She told me of her physical affairs. She flaunted her body at me. She laughed at me and tried to create in me a desire for her flesh. She spoke of my sister, her mother, and inferred that the relationship between us had been diseased, unnatural. I knelt on sharp stones for hours at a time, praying for guidance. I had begun to desire her and I could not cut that evil longing out of my heart."

In the beginning he had spoken tersely, factually. Now his voice had deepened and there was almost a biblical cadence in his words.

"When she would go away I would begin to heal myself, but on her return I would turn again to paths of error. At last she taunted me with the affair she was having with a married man, Dodd Raymond, son of old friends. She taunted me with that as she had taunted me with vile details of her affair with young Yeagger. She wished to punish me for the fancied cruelties I had practiced on her when she was younger. She spoke of a rented place where she would meet Raymond. I saw that she would spend her life spreading her own kind of evil. I told her her father had been evil and he had died. She looked at me then with a special kind of recognition. Maybe my face had shown her too much. I knew that she had begun to suspect me. I knew then that she would have to die also. Once I had decided it, I felt cleansed.

"When my family went to the lake a week ago last Saturday, a week ago yesterday, I parked near the Locust Ridge Club and followed her in her car when she left. I thought she was with Raymond. I thought they would go to the rented place she spoke of. I followed them until they turned into a driveway in the old part of the city. To make certain, I turned around and went back and turned into the driveway. My headlights were on them and I saw them clearly in carnal embrace. I returned to my home to wait for her. I expected her to be very late. She came sooner than I expected. As with her father, I mercifully decided to give her a last chance. I told her I wished to talk to her.

"She listened for a long time, quite patiently. I told her how she had to combat the evil she had inherited. I spoke calmly to her. When I was through she laughed at me. She jeered at me and said unforgivable things to me. I walked away from the car, trembling. I went in the house and took a sock from my bedroom and went out and filled the toe with coarse dirt. When she came walking toward the house, humming to herself, I struck her as hard as I could, caught her as she fell and put her back in the car.

"I thought for a long time. Raymond had broken vows. I found a strange key in her purse. I drove back to the apartment, left her in the car. The key opened the door. I went in and found him in bed, breathing heavily, smelling of drink. I struck him twice, as hard as I could, to prevent his awakening. In the darkness his head was clearly visible on the pillow. His breathing changed and that was all. I carried her into the dark apartment. She seemed to have no weight at all. I placed her in the closet. I lighted a match and saw a belt hanging there. I placed it around her neck and drew it tight. I knelt in the closet doorway in the darkness. I could hear a faint whistle of breathing. I tightened the belt a bit more and I could hear nothing.

"I waited a long time and began to tremble. I thrust her further back into the closet, closed the door, closed the outside door and drove away. I did not sleep that night. Early in the morning I called my wife at the lake and said that Mary had not come home and I was worried. Myrna drove down from the lake. It was minutes before she arrived that I happened to see Mary's purse near the edge of the drive where I had struck her. . . ."

"The car, her car," Kruslov said softly.

"I drove her car from Sewell's driveway and abandoned it near Highland. I walked two miles to the farm and drove back to my home in one of the jeeps. I rubbed my hands on the parts of her car I had touched, to smear my fingerprints. I hid her purse and the key in my bureau. After my wife returned from the lake and we phoned Stine, I waited for Raymond to be found with the body in that apartment. We told Stine that Mary had been at the club with the Raymonds. But it turned out I had struck Sewell. When the body was not found, I guessed that Sewell had taken it away somehow. I did not want Sewell punished. I suspected that he and Mary had been intimate, but I had no proof.

"I wanted to talk to Sewell, to find out if he too should be punished. I waited one night near his apartment, the night Mary's body had been found. He drove in with Yeagger. I was behind a tree. They came close to me and fought. I got a tire iron from my car. Yeagger was choking Sewell. I struck him from behind. I thought I had killed him. Sewell still breathed. I left.

"Sewell's arrest troubled me. I visited him in his cell. He seemed honest. He disclaimed carnal knowledge of my niece. I was afraid that once again, as with Nadine, the innocent would be punished. I began to think of confession and suicide. I was the instrument of the vengeance of the Lord, but He did not want me to punish the innocent.

"When Raymond phoned me to set a place to speak to me in private, I had no idea what he wanted. I had him meet me at the farm on Friday night. He spoke cautiously. Suddenly I realized what he wanted. Mary had hinted of her suspicions that perhaps I had killed her father. She had told him of the relationship between herself and me. Raymond had a business venture in mind. I would furnish funds. He said he could insure a good return. Otherwise he would go to the police with his suspicions, and he felt there would be enough to warrant reopening the investigation. I told him I would have to think it over. I told him to wait there. He showed me the gun he was carrying.

"I went back to my home and recovered Mary's purse from its hiding place and took it back out there with me. The sock heavy with dirt had worked so well that I used it another time. It did not take long to catch him off guard. I spoke of large sums of money and his greed diluted his caution. He was a heavy man, but as when I carried Mary, he seemed astonishingly light. I removed my shoes so as not to leave telltale marks on the roof of his car. The most difficult part was holding him upright while I knotted the tow line around his neck. He began to recover consciousness as I held him upright. I put the purse in one side pocket and the key in the other.

"I pushed him off the car. He caught at the rope over his head with his hands and when he swung back he scrabbled at the car roof with his feet but he could not get a purchase. On the second swing he did not come close enough. He held his weight with his hands, swinging and turning slowly. I had used a flashlight to locate the proper limb and judge the throw. I turned the light on him. He swung, turning slowly, looking at me with a terrible face. I turned off the light. I put my shoes on and stood by the car in the darkness. Soon I heard the sounds of his dying. I walked back to the farm and drove home. I knew it was all over. Sewell would be freed. The guilty had been punished. I felt clean again, as in the moment when I decided to kill my niece.

"When Sewell spoke to me today my anger turned me blind. I knew that it was all over in a different sense. I was angered because I had saved him and this was the way he would repay me."

Pryor stood up slowly. The faces of the listeners changed. The orange fountain pen made a tiny scratching sound as the last few words were taken down.

Pryor turned toward Kruslov. "Now that you know all the reasons, Captain, now that I have explained everything in detail, may I go home? I'll appreciate it if this is given no publicity."

I swear that Kruslov was so shocked he almost said yes. He licked his lips and said, "Oh no, Mr. Pryor! You can't go home."

"Do you plan to detain me? Here?"

"I'm afraid I've got to."

"Well, get your formalities over as soon as possible then. Will I be able to go home this evening?"

I saw the Kruslov brain begin to tick. He stood up and smiled and said, "Mr. Pryor, rest assured that we'll take care of all this just as efficiently as we know how. If you'll come along with me, sir?"

They half bowed to each other. As they went out the door together, Willis Pryor said, "Remember now. No publicity. And I'd like to talk to Jud Sutton as soon as possible. Get him for me, please."

"Right this way, Mr. Pryor," Kruslov said gently.

We were all left in the room. Somebody sighed. Then we all filed out of there, not looking at each other. We all shared some nameless guilt. We'd all seen the shining structures fall, the streets decay, the walls crumble. We didn't want anything to do with each other. Maybe we had all resigned from the human race a little bit.

Young John Olan was standing in the main corridor when I left. Nobody seemed to want me, so I left. A reporter had edged up to me and I had snarled at him. John Olan was studying a pocket chessboard.

"More prepared variations?"

I startled him. He recognized me and smiled at me. "That's right."

He jerked his head toward the other end of the corridor, the official end. "He did it? My father and my sister?"

"Yes. I'm sorry."

His eyes were dark mirrors, reflecting nothing. His

mouth moved in a quick grimace of pain, wiped out immediately.

He looked back at the board in his hand. I no longer existed. He was back in a special clean geometric world, where the god was reason, where the goddess was logic, where hearts were prisms, cold and true and neatly cut. Perhaps it was a good world to hide in.

I left him and walked slowly to my car in the late afternoon sunshine. A thunder front was rolling up the sky, and the sun was beginning to be misted, and the city was full of an orange light, lambent and ominous.

chapter 11

I missed Dodd's funeral. Toni drove me out to the airport in my car and I caught flight 818 to New York at one twenty P.M. on Monday, in accordance with the terse telegram I had received.

BE IN MY OFFICE AT FIVE THIRTY TODAY
STACE

I went in no mood of capitulation, with no humility, with rather a well banked anger that burned dull and low under the covering coals.

It was a close thing. I went from Kennedy into heavy traffic and got out of the cab in front of the C.P.P. building on Madison near Fiftieth at twenty after five.

The elevator banks were disgorging their full quota of the sharp-eyed girls from the offices. The big sepia photomural of the Fall River plant above the directory, across from the elevators, looked just the same. The main offices specialize, through handling and atmosphere, in dwarfing you. A boulder in the field, you become a pebble in a shoe when you hit the topside offices.

I was alone on my ride up to the hushed beige splendor of eighteenth floor reception. A soft-voiced duchess, all prepared to leave her upholstered nest for the day, focused eighteen inches over my head, lifted a forest green phone from the beige formica of a free-form display desk and confirmed my appointment with a rusty little accent that was entirely delicious. I said I knew where to go and, the barometer of my spirits dropping steadily, I trudged back through lesser sanctums to the corner office where a golden girl opened the two-inch-thick door to let me in. Homer Stace, Executive Vice-President in Charge of Production, Member of the Board, sat thick and secure with his back to all the glass and a segment of the river, and a distant tug with colors sharp and bright against afternoon smog.

"Sit down, Sewell," he said. Mr. Stace is a big florid man who started with grease on his hands. Along the way he cultivated ersatz British mannerisms, a look of spurious stupidity, a bumbling jolly manner. He delights in being underestimated. He's as sharp as a Chicago ice-pick.

Not for me the window dressing, the mannerisms, the jolly bumbling. For me the cold eye, glacial, unearthed somewhere in Greenland and imported frozen in a block of mercury.

I sat.

"What kind of an outrage is going on out there? Exactly what the hell are we taking on these days? Playboys? Sex maniacs? Since when does a responsible position with C.P.P. become window dressing for a night-life career, Sewell? You young social lions sicken me. What kind of stupid God damn reason can you think of to convince me that I ought to keep you on the payroll, even to scrub washrooms?"

It worked like an air injection system. It turned on the blower under my banked fire. I stopped sitting. I stood up and slammed both fists down on his desk top.

"What makes you think I want to stay on your damn payroll?"

He came right up to meet me, nose to nose. "People like you are a dime a dozen, Sewell."

"Don't classify me, damn it."

"I suppose you're unique!" He bawled that with the monstrous arrogance of a rhino.

"Yes!"

"Irreplaceable?"

"Yes!" I hit his desk again. "I don't have to work for this outfit. I can work for anybody. I'll do all right."

We glared at each other. His voice changed. "Sit down, damn it," he said softly. We both sat down. He made a quarter turn on his big chair, took a mint out of his desk drawer, tossed it into his mouth, turned a bit further and looked out his special window. I looked at the back of his thick stubborn neck.

Finally he grunted to his feet, crossed to the corner of the office, opened a cabinet and took out a bottle of Irish whisky, half full. He raised it and one eyebrow. "With water," I said.

He took the ice from a small gas refrigerator with a walnut finish. He made two generous drinks and brought them back, gave me one, spat what was left of his mint into a leather wastebasket.

"Skoal."

"Skoal."

He took his sweet time, never looking directly at me. Finally he said, "Sewell, what do you think happens to the young men who are so obviously perfect C.P.P. material?"

"They get to be president some day. The hell with them."

He took another sip. "Bad guess. They do all right. They get to be plant managers. And they head up various sections. They retire with pleasant pensions and have charming grandchildren."

"So?"

"Now what happens to the mavericks?"

"You fire them personally."

He nodded. "I fire a lot of them. A lot of them leave and go with other outfits. We manage to keep a very few. We have to."

"Why? For comic relief?"

"Because we eventually need them for top management. To lean on the plant managers, the section heads and all the other 'almosts.' Something is wrong with our system, Sewell, with the whole system throughout industry of selecting men and promoting them for those very traits which prevent their reaching the real top—the peak of the hill where it's damn cold, tough and lonely. For our future success we need to retain, nurture, cherish a few of the offbeat types. Like you."

"I beg your pardon."

"You aren't going to get much chance to rest, Sewell. I'm personally going to drive hell out of you. If I make it too rough you can leave, and the hell with you."

"Look, I . . ."

"Shut up a minute. In five years, if you last, I'm bringing you in here. Then it will really get rugged. You'll go back there into Raymond's job."

"Thanks."

He looked at me sourly. "Do you mean that?"

"Not entirely. I earned it."

"You also earned having the can tied to you."

"I know that too."

"Finish your drink."

I finished it and stood up. We shook hands. He had a smug satisfied gleam in his eye. I realized with surprise that I could even get to like the bastard.

When I reached his office door I looked back. He was looking out his window.

"By the way, I'm marrying my secretary."

He didn't move or turn. "I don't care if you marry a cretin cleaning woman. All I want out of you is fourteen hours a day."

I shut the door harder than I had to. Tory had waited. I gave him the full report. We got drunk. He put me on a midnight plane. I was at the plant at eight-twenty on Tuesday morning. I married MacRae the following Saturday. We're going to live at Brookways until they move us to the next town.